THE VENGEANCE
OF THE GODS

AMS PRESS
NEW YORK

THE VENGEANCE
OF THE GODS

AND THREE OTHER STORIES OF REAL
AMERICAN COLOR LINE LIFE

By WILLIAM PICKENS

Author of "The Heir of Slaves," "The New Negro," Etc.

Introduction by

Bishop John Hurst, D.D., LL.D.
of the African Methodist Episcopal Church

PUBLISHED BY
THE A. M. E. BOOK CONCERN
631 PINE STREET
PHILADELPHIA, PA.

Library of Congress Cataloging in Publication Data

Pickens, William, 1881-1954.
    The vengeance of the gods, and three other stories of
real American color line life.

    Reprint of the 1922 ed. published by A. M. E. Book
Concern, Philadelphia.
    CONTENTS: The vengeance of the gods.—The superior
race.—Passing the buck.—Tit for tat.
    I. Title.
PZ3.P5853Vell [PS3531.I263]   813'.5'2   73-18564
ISBN 0-404-11376-1

Trim size of AMS edition of this book is 5 x 6 7/8.
Original edition is 5 1/2 x 7 7/8

Reprinted from the edition of 1922, Philadelphia
First AMS edition published in 1975
Manufactured in the United States of America

AMS PRESS INC.
NEW YORK, N.Y.

INTRODUCTION
By Bishop John Hurst

One of the hardest things in the world to accom‑ plish is to get rid of a fixed idea. The fixed idea frequently is the lunacy of otherwise sane minds. When good, it is beneficial in its workings. When evil, it is destructive and the injuries it commits know no bounds.

The fact that a man differs in physical traits from another does not establish his superiority. Things external in human relations have but scant value. The refining and spiritualizing forces are those that count. It is a tremendously big price to pay if, in order to prove his superiority, a fellow has to resort to sharp practices, immoral schemes and brutalizing standards. He is deteriorating without knowing it. Germany aimed for a com‑ manding position in the world through material success and military and individual efficiency. Her leaders were obsessed with the idea of proving by those means their superiority over everybody else. They started as if to say, in effect, "Watch us put it over. See whether we do not build up a model system producing the finest result attained anywhere in commerce and industry—whether we do not make Germany the leader of modern civ‑ ilization—the most powerful nation ever known to man." It took them fifty years to put the scheme through, but they woke up to find all of it but illusions and short-sightedness. Now they are being un-educated from this foible, from this false conception of life. There is hope for them.

But the process of un-educating one's self from old habits and false notions and prejudices of many centuries is most difficult. People thus affected are frequently found reversing themselves. It is a work of slow growth and almost interminable. They need light and more of it every day. Writers who devote their talent in furnishing material to meet this condition render double service: they help the blind out of his dungeon and build up hope and expectation of a brighter day in the breast of the sufferer. They are entitled to the encouragement and respect of those whom they serve. The colored people must learn more and more to support them and, by that means, hasten the dawn of the social and spiritual redemption of mankind.

This small volume of stories explodes in a vivacious and engaging style, for which its author is so well known, the false philosophic and scientific value of the doctrine of Race Superiority and the way it demonstrates itself. The author points out with great appositeness the base and abject level to which its advocates and patrons will descend to maintain and prove their thesis, but, invariably, with sinister results to themselves. We believe and trust that it will meet with a hearty welcome by all.

CONTENTS

FOREWORD

Painter and Picture

Who paints the picture, paints himself beautiful. Colored people often complain that in American literature the Negro characters are made either hideous or undesirable or unheroic. The colored people did not make that literature. People do not present another race as beautiful and heroic, unless that race is far removed from them in time or space; or unless, as in the case of the white man and the American Indian, the stronger race has killed off the weaker and removed it as a rival. The 20th century white man can speak romantically of the Indians,—of Indian courage, Indian war and Indian love. But to the 18th century white man, whom the Indian menaced from the neighboring plains, there was "no good Indian but a dead Indian."

If the Negro wants to be idealized in a world where the Negro is a considerable potential factor, he must idealize himself,—or else he must expect a sorry role in every tale from "Mother Goose" to Wells' "Outline of History." It is not simply that the white story teller *will not* do full justice to the humanity of the black race; he *cannot*. A race must present its own case and ennoble its own ideals.

The custom of representing the Negro in story as either a clown or a villain, or else a faithful and useful servant to some white person, has been so universal that even the earlier Negro writers dared not venture beyond it, especially when they were dependent upon white publishers. The colored writer is now beginning to present his race unapologetically and with the full attributes of MAN.

When the small boy saw on the walls of his home a painting representing a man as mastering and subduing with his bare hands a strong lion, the child asked: "Mother, how can *that* man whip the lion so easily? Every time I read about lions in Africa or see them at the circus, hundreds of people are afraid of one lion." His mother gave him the full explanation: "My son, it is like this: those lions did not paint that picture."

But we are not writing an essay on story-telling; we are simply presenting to the reader the four stories of this little book, with the statement that the colored characters are so completely human that some people would consider them unnatural.

The first is "The Vengeance of the Gods." The author must do most of such work on the road and in railway trains,—on his knee in Jim Crow cars or on a table in Pullman. This particular story was written on a circle tour of the far west. The first chapter was written in Spokane, Washington, and the last in Indianapolis, Indiana; the intervening chapters or parts of them in Tacoma, Portland, Sacramento, Oakland, San Francisco, San Jose, Vallejo, Los Angeles, San Diego, Phoenix, Albuquerque, El Paso and other points in Texas, and in Arkansas. It recalls many of the author's boyhood recollections of the peonage-infested districts of the last named state.

The second story, "The Superior Race," was written after the author had had a considerable sea voyage. The scene is laid in Mobile Bay and the Gulf of Mexico, and is built around an incident that was related to him.

The third story, "Passing the Buck," was originally called "Trapped." It contains incidents which will be remembered by many people who attended the great Methodist Centenary Celebration in Columbus, Ohio, 1919. It was written one morning in a Pullman car crossing the desert of the Dakotas and Wyoming.

The last story, "Tit for Tat," relates what actually happened in the life of a colored regiment from Illinois while it was seeing service in France. The substance of this story was given me by a former high officer of that regiment in a conversation at the Appomattox Club in Chicago.

All of these stories are facts and types, but not of the kind that the white American will yet be enthusiastic about printing, although he may read them.   WILLIAM PICKENS
260 W. 139th St., New York, N. Y.

THE VENGEANCE OF THE GODS

Blood or Opportunity?

CHAPTER I.

"TWO TWINS"

There is an old unsettled war 'twixt blood and chance. Heredity or environment? Which has the major influence on the destinies of men?

The unnatural social and the illegitimate sex relations of white and colored people in the United States furnish the best body of material through which to investigate this problem. One of the best illustrations of the power of environment and at the same time the persistency of blood, hails from the river lands of the State of Arkansas.

John Elliot was a wealthy plantation owner. He held title to many thousand acres of fertile cotton lands of eastern Arkansas in the last decade of the nineteenth century. His farms were worked by scores of Negro families, most of whom had migrated from the Carolinas and Georgia in the eighties. Elliot had advanced the railroad fares to these families through his labor agents who operated in the older states. The heads of these families had "made their mark" or signed their names to contracts for their entire families to "work out" these debts on Elliot's estate. These contracts were made and signed through agents in the older states, and the "parties of the second part" had no knowledge of the conditions of the work to be required, beyond the general understanding that it was farm labor.

Of course, Elliot had to furnish these "newcomers" their "rations." For most of them came west in the winter, after the close of the farming season in the east; and accordingly they had to be supplied with food and clothing at the expense of the new landlord even before steady work should begin in the spring. This caused the debt against them to mount rapidly, for the landlord charged these supplies to their account at a profit to himself of one hundred per cent or more. And although he was party to the contract, he was sole keeper of all records; and it was not necessary to tell the consumer what he was being charged for a gallon of molasses till the final settlement next fall or Christmas,—and not necessary then.

This system was the successor and heir of the slave system. Elliot lived in "the Big House" on a long and ample hill near the center of his estates, while the Negroes lived in cabins of one or two rooms, all over the great plantations, each cabin being situated on or near the little farm that was assigned or allotted to its occupants. Once each month, on the regular "rationing day," all the

heads of these various tenant or peon families came
to the Big House to claim as much molasses, salt
pork, meal, dark-brown sugar, coffee and rice as
was deemed necessary to keep their respective
families alive for thirty days more. This system
kept them tied close to their master and periodical-
ly reminded of their dependence upon him.

The landlord was perfectly secure in these advanced outlays: the tenant was bound by this debt
and local law would enforce it against his very
person, spite of the Thirteenth Amendment. If he
sought to escape, any justice of the peace could
fine him and then jail him in default of payment
of fine. But of course the fine would be paid by
his magnanimous and benevolent (?) landlord and
added to his former debt,—thus binding him the
closer. In fact it was better for the landlord when a
peon attempted to escape and failed, for after the
matter was reviewed by the "court" or justice, it
gave the aggrieved landlord a better claim, a sort
of adjudicated title to this Negro's brawn.

Thus the original "cost of transportation" from
South Carolina to Arkansas became an octopus
with ever increasing bulk and multiplying suckers.
Despair broke many a heart. Even the doctor and
his medicines had to be secured through this system. Chills and fevers attacked the unacclimated
new-comers and they had to summon the plantation doctor, who got his pay, not from the tenant,
but from the great land-baron, who in turn charged

this account against the tenant's account at the Big House,—with the usual profits. This doctor who was not at all accountable to the tenant, naturally gave himself the least trouble: he might ride to the door of a cabin where black people lay fevered and delirious within, and without dismounting from his saddle make a few inquiries, write a prescription for medicine, hand it down and ride away.

Small wonder that under circumstances such as these some of the more thrifty and determined immigrants would try auxiliary means to break the bonds of this gripping debt-slavery,—even allowing their women folk to serve as cooks or maids or washerwomen to the white folk in the Big House and elsewhere.

And this is how "Aunt Katy," now a woman of middle age, had come into the family of John Elliot as a maid-of-all-work. Twenty years before, when she was a slim black girl of twenty, she and her father and mother and younger sisters and brothers had become the debt-slaves of John Elliot. They were of those wonderfully virile black folk of South Carolina, whose mark can be found everywhere in America today. They escaped from the barren poverty of their native state to find themselves in the rich cotton lands of the great Arkansas "bottoms,'" but also in the coils of the octopus. All hands worked with a will, even the little children being deprived of most of their schooling. The oldest sister, Katy, was hired out as house girl to the Elliots, lords of the estate. "Aunt Katy," a title which the dignity and the burden of more years had finally won for her, was now a matronly-looking black woman with a bit of gray about her temples. She had that clear and beautiful black skin through which the red blood was visible on the more prominent features of the face.

Aunt Katy had a daughter, Essie, who should not be described as yellow, but as of a rich cream color decorated with vanishing rose tints, which sometimes appear in the sun-lit eddies when the powerful streams of black and white run into the same channel.

And Essie, only nineteen years old, had a baby, with dark hair, dark eyes, and skin—*white*.

Three generations: mother, daughter, grandson —black, light, white. And yet, in law, they were all black; and in the wisdom of the same law Essie, Aunt Katy's daughter, had no father, and Essie's baby was fatherless.

And yet the stranger, to whom resemblances are always more discernible, might have noticed that although these two normal human creatures were legally akin to nobody, they very much resembled some of their neighbors. Essie was enough like Mrs. Elliot, the wife of the landlord, to be her daughter; and Mrs. Elliot's baby looked like the twin of Essie's baby. These little baby boys were six months old and just ten days apart in their birth, the Elliot baby being the older. And they were indeed so indistinguishably alike that one day Mrs. Elliot, seeing Essie's baby clad in the cast-off clothes of her own child, seized it in her arms, and pressing it to her heart she inquired of Aunt Katy pettishly: "Why have you put my little angel into these old rags? I told you to throw them away."

"That's Essie's—not your'n!" said Aunt Katy, in a tone not altogether kind. Mrs. Elliot almost dropped the child into Aunt Katy's arms. Mrs. Elliot had heard all about this child and knew well the circumstances of its being. But this moment of realization seemed to arouse the jungle woman. She looked wrathfully toward John Elliot, who sat in his easy chair, spying upon the scene through the smoke screen of his pipe. He was the picture of self-satisfaction and conscious mastery. And when his angry mate turned upon him, all the threatening storm of her sex gathered itself in this one harmless bolt:

"As God lives, no good will ever come of this!" To which John Elliot replied with a new cloud of smoke, as if to thicken the screen and dodge any second shot.

Then, as too frequently happens in such cases, this indignant wife turned all her anger and fury away from the really guilty party and upon his helpless victims:

"And this is *thanks*, is it, **Katy**?" forgetting the mollifying Southern term of "Aunt."—"We gave you work and bread when my only brother was here,—and there is Essie. And now *this* from her, and she my brother's own ————!"

She stopped short and shook with wrath. The code of honor of her group forbade to speak plainly and honorably her relationship to these people. But Essie was her natural niece, her own brother's child; and Essie's baby was the half-brother and apparently the very twin of her own child. These plain things her proud tongue could not utter, but the following came natural to her:

"You niggers all! Take those clothes off that brat, and never bring your daughter or this thing near my house again. Let Essie work on the farm, and we have plenty of coarse cloth for nigger children."

With that she swept proudly away. John Elliot had already withdrawn to the porch.

Meanwhile dark rage and the images of darker resolves were sweeping the dusky breast of Aunt Katy, like the shadows of storm clouds. She remembered how twenty years ago she was practically trapped and assaulted by this woman's pampered brother, and how this very woman had excused and connived, and was certainly an accomplice after the fact. And now Essie, the fruit and one of the victims of the previous wrong, had told her mother how this white woman's own husband had at first attempted to take advantage of her through bribery and persuasion and coercion; and failing in that, had finally used force to do this thing.

And yet, continued Aunt Katy's memory, this woman had kept her and her child Essie for twenty years in the Big House. A few weeks before Essie's baby was born, Mrs. Elliot had ordered Aunt Katy to put the prospective mother into one of the servant's cabins; whereupon Aunt Katy had also moved out to live with Essie although she still performed her daily tasks at the Elliot's. The baby had been born, and everybody had remarked that it was "the very spit an' image uv ole man Elliot." The colored people said that Essie's baby and Mrs. Elliot's baby were as much alike "as two black-eyed peas."

Time had passed, and Essie began again to go back and forth from the cabin to the Big House to assist in the work. Aunt Katy who spent most of her time in and near the kitchen and dining room, kept the little grandchildren with her. Under the strange power which the evils we tolerate seem to acquire over us, Mrs. Elliot had apparently become reconciled to all this, and Essie was as formerly her hair-dresser and maid. But the mistress was less communicative, somewhat less condescending and much more formal in her relations with this beautiful outcaste creature, and always dismissed her now as soon as the work was finished.

In a few moments all this record unrolled itself in Aunt Katy's heated brain. And it would not have comforted the Elliots, had they remained to observe the fire of her dark deep African eyes. She hugged passionately the little nameless grandchild, which, though frightened for the moment by the storm that had passed with Mrs. Elliot, was still unconscious of its own situation and immune against the deeper significance of all these clashing forces, and was now pressing its soft baby cheek against the dark face of its grandmother and patting her neck with a tiny hand.

"No!" exclaimed Aunt Katy, in apostrophizing defiance, "my Essie will not work in your fields." Then hugging the baby closer: "You will not be put among strangers. You an' Essie can stay in the cabin; I will support you." And looking in the direction toward which Mrs. Elliot had gone: "What can *she* do without me? I have cared for her house for twenty years.—Yes, long as I live, he will support you, and Essie too. For if they refuse to support you in the cabin ————" Her tongue refused to utter the awful thought which seemed to find it difficult to express itself even in the sudden demon look of her face. This terrible inspiration ran into a dry, jerky, inhuman laugh, which so frightened the child that it clung the closer about her neck.

CHAPTER II.

THE TATTOO AND THE SCAR

THE TATTOO

Miss Ollie Price, Mrs. Elliot's younger sister, who since her school-days had led the life of a social "climber," and almost that of an adventuress in the east, had at last become engaged to some French sportsman, and was now back at her sister's home in Arkansas to prepare for the wedding. She needed a maid, she must have a maid. That was what everybody had in New York and Washington. Mrs. Elliot told her that on all the Elliot plantations there was but one person qualified for the position,—Aunt Katy's daughter Essie. Then she related to her sister all the circumstances connected with Essie's banishment to the cabin. Miss Price who had experienced some liberalizing contact with the outside world, replied that it was "too bad," and even referred to Essie as "the poor thing." But then she "must have a suitable maid."

Essie was accordingly recalled from her exile to serve again at the Big House. Expedience is master of many of our emotions and author of many of our decisions.

Curiosity led "Miss Ollie" to seek an opportunity to see Essie's baby. One day while Essie was arranging her new Mistress' hair, Miss Price was contemplating the face and figure of the beautiful mulatto in her mirror. And perhaps tenderness was vying with curiosity when she said: "It must be hard to leave your baby so long. Bring him with you tomorrow, and I think—you will work better."

"But, Miss Ollie, Mis' Elliot ————."

"O, that's all right," anticipated Miss Price, "It'll be all right in my rooms." And then with a tone almost of command: "Bring him tomorrow."

The next day Miss Price was surprised almost into speechlessness by the closeness of resemblance between this child and her own little nephew. She was agitated. By a strange fascination we often seek after what will not comfort us. "What is his name?" she asked Essie, as the little fellow traced with his finger the figures in the wall paper opposite her.

"We call him Jim," said Essie, blushing and uncomfortable.

"Jim!" called Miss Price, as if to test the matter or to destroy a possible illusion. The little fellow shrank at the strange voice, turned timidly and moved around in the direction of its mother.

Her own nephew would run to her at the slightest invitation.

The sure instincts of the mother caught the meaning of all this curious interest. She was pensive and pale and silent as she worked all that morning, and little Jim also gave the stranger lady a wide berth when he moved about the room, as if sympathetic with his mother's spirit. When she went away at noon she did not bring him back, and she remarked that he was right out in the kitchen with "Aunt Katy," as she called her own mother, where she could see him when necessary. It did not escape her notice that Miss Price now made no protest against his absence, and never asked to see him and never even mentioned the child again. It is hard to be consistent in a false attitude.

Miss Price talked much about this child, however, to her sister, Mrs. Elliot: "Suppose something should happen! How could you make sure? Only their clothes make it possible to tell one from the other."

"Nonsense!" retorted the proud white mother, "because you have been staying in the North, you forget the difference between a white person and a nigger. If the nails or the hair of the neck don't tell, the very spirit will tell. Blood will tell! Why, if they were lost till they were grown, you could tell the white man and the nigger when you found them."

But Miss Price was nonetheless skeptic. She disclosed to her sister that she had learned from a sailor associate in the east the art of tattooing, and shocked that lady's honor and offended her pride of race by proposing to tattoo little nephew William as a distinguishing mark. As proof of her skill she showed on her left arm a small tattoo which she herself had done. The haughty wife and proud mother rejected this proposal with an air that was truly impressive of her faith in racial superiority and "blood."

But that one sight of little Jim had stuck like poison in Miss Price's soul. She could be seen often brooding and gazing into the far-away when playing with nephew William. She was trying to prevail upon her sister to permit her to take the child to France after the wedding. Meanwhile Mrs. Elliot and her husband were summoned to the bedside of her brother, the natural father of Essie, who was dying in Atlanta. Miss Price readily consented to assume the responsibility for the household and the care of her little nephew. The Elliots were gone for several weeks, what with funeral arrangements and what with looking after the brother's estate.

If Mrs. Elliot had ever bathed and dressed her own baby instead of leaving it entirely to the servants, she might have noticed, when she returned from Atlanta, a mark under its arm up near the body. This mark was irregular in shape but might have passed for an M or a W, accordingly as one looked at it. But with her sublime confidence in herself and her kind, she noticed nothing. And the servants, who had been glad to have "Miss Ollie" to relieve them of all service to little "Willyum" for several weeks, saw nothing—and cared not.

THE SCAR

The wedding came to pass. The Elliots were persuaded to take the trip to France with the bride and groom. It was arranged to take Essie along as maid to the whole party. She would return with the Elliots, who would stay about three months. Mrs. Elliot had consented to go only after her sister in New Orleans agreed to come and be the head of the place in their absence and take care of the child. And Essie had been reconciled to going only after it was agreed that her own mother, Aunt Katy, should have entire care of "Jimmie." The Elliots also had every confidence in Aunt Katy, but then it "would look better to have some white person in charge here." That is a religion in the South. Aunt Katy would be the real head and the chief reliance. Indeed nothing could have induced Mrs. Elliot to leave her child or her house in the care of even her own sister without the help of Aunt Katy. But altho a colored person may be the *defacto* head, the *de jure* headship must reside in a "white person."

This New Orleans sister could not come, however, until some time after the wedding party had left, and before the Elliots and Duprees set sail from New York, they received the anxiously awaited news of her arrival. She reported that all was well at the Big House and that Aunt Katy had taken excellent care of the interests of the Elliots. She had met the new arrival and brought little William in her arms, who was "the very picture of health, and, O. so fond of Aunt Katy," as the letter went on to say.

What had really happened was this: when this strange aunt arrived, the child in Aunt Katy's arms would have nothing to do with the newcomer but clung with both arms tight around the black woman's neck, its cheek against her cheek. The child seemed frightened when the stranger touched it and showed no disposition to respond to her repeated invitations to "my dearest little nephew William." The chagrined aunt did not relate all this in her letter, for indeed she felt ashamed to tell in detail of the very cold reception accorded her by the heir to the Elliot estate. Pride deals in half truths and camouflage. She went on to say that she hoped soon to win the entire confidence and affection of the little master of the place, altho they were strangers for the present and she was allowing him to sleep with Aunt Katy.

At this point in the letter, the former Miss

Price who was now Madame Dupree, parted her lips and gasped and was about to make some earnest comment,—but subsided when the next line went on to say:

"Do not tell Essie that a little accident happened to Jimmie. He was burned the next day after you left. He was not seriously hurt, but the doctor says it will leave a large scar on his leg.

"Aunt Katy says it happend in the kitchen. The child pulled a hot stove lid down. Fortunately William was not around, as Aunt Katy had sent him out for a ride with the new nurse who came that same day."

The letter repeated and emphasized it as a request from Aunt Katy "not to tell Essie about it," and said that the grandmother was much distressed. This last statement seemed to produce a complete calm in Madame Dupree's features, and she only remarked: "Aunt Katy always would have that young one hanging to her apron in the kitchen." Then, as if to reassure herself: "And did she say that it is the doctor's opinion that the scar on the leg will last for life?"

CHAPTER III.

THE DEMOCRACY OF BABYHOOD

There is one perfect spirit of equality in this world,—in babyhood. Titles, ancestors, blood, wealth and social circles are not esteemed by babies. Feature and color and caste do not vex the social life of babydom.

Little William and little Jimmie were in their second year of life. With their parents far over the sea, and with their guardians, Aunt Katy and "Auntie," equally as far way, so far as the babies were concerned, being in distant parts of the Big House,—the two little fellows were enjoying each other's society in the great dining room, without reserve. Jimmie was dressed in home-made ginghams and his feet were bare. An ugly scar of the recent burn could be seen on his otherwise perfect baby leg. William was dressed in blue serge, trimmed in white, with blue-and-white socks and black pumps.

William selected the rag doll, which Aunt Katy had made for Jimmie, seated it in the best chair of his doll furniture set, and was feeding "M'randa" some "soogar" out of a silver spoon.

Jimmie in the meanwhile had the blue-eyed, linen-clad, frilled-up French doll which Aunt Ollie had given William, and was trying to compel this well-dressed foreigner to do the menial work of shoveling the dirt from the dust pan into a teacup. A large pot spoon longer than the doll was the "shubble." And as the frilled-up Frenchman seemed not to take hold enthusiastically and to be unappreciative of the dignity of labor, Jimmie was occasionally pulling its blond hair and slapping its face until its blue eyes shook, while he lectured in the best baby Brobdingnagian style.

After William's rag doll protege had indeed much more sugar on the outside than on the inside,—as much of that article was sticking in grains about its mouth and piled in heaps in its lap and on the floor, in the manner of real babies, —William remembered to hang a napkin about its dingy neck. He was much kinder to this rag baby than was Jimmie to the fashionable Frenchman. Adjusting the napkin, he next placed on "M'randa's" lap a table spoon and an individual butter dish running over with "soogar." Completing this pacifying arrangement, he rose to his feet, grabbed the coarse bonnet which belonged to Jimmie, and placed it on his own head. He then turned toward his playmate, who was still busily employing extreme but ineffectual measures to industrialize the aristocratic Frenchman, and beating the air with his hands, he uttered, in sharp accents which sounded like a series of commands, the following vocals:

"Ah! ah! oo—oo—oo—oo! ee—eeh!"

Whatever all that may mean in the secret codes of babyhood, Jimmie understood it instantly and perfectly. He looked up, and jumped from his corner, dropping the indocile Frenchman into the dirt of the dust pan. Then he ran and picked up the cream-colored, blue-ribboned sailor hat which belonged to William, and put it on his own head. Hand-in-hand they now turned toward the door and were just about to sally forth to some great baby adventure, when in came William's New Orleans Aunt facing them like an angry fairy:

"William!" —— and then she stopped, turned to stone, as it were, by the sight which she beheld: two little playmates in perfect accord and brotherhood, with not a thought of difference or caste; William with his linens under Jimmie's coarse bonnet and Jimmie with his ginghams under William's trim sailor.

The next reaction of the sophisticated grown-up was violent. She flung the bonnet from William's head and jerked the sailor from the head of Jimmie. And again she was turned to stone when those two heads were disclosed: they were so much alike, evidently from the same mold. She looked at the scar on Jimmie's leg and muttered something about "providence." What conceit it is that makes us believe that supernatural powers are allied with our littlenesses. Both children recoiled before her scrutiny. Her own nephew still preferred Aunt Katy at times, which somewhat annoyed his aunt. The likeness of these two babies had never before impressed her so deeply. In her curiosity she took hold of Jimmie, turned him round and round, looked alternately from him to William, and examined the scar again. She pushed up the wide gingham sleeves of the puzzled little fellow, looking ever and anon toward William. And finally, fixing her eyes for a moment on something under Jimmie's arm, she muttered: "A birthmark also."

Then leading little William with one hand and carrying his defiled sailor hat in the other, she went out of the dining room toward the parlors, leaving Jimmie as if he were no longer in existence. The latter instinctively resented this slight by kicking over the rag doll and spilling her plate of sugar, after which he pulled the napkin from her neck and stood holding her by one leg as if contemplating some much more terrible reprisals.

The New Orleans Aunt had not been conscious of the dark face that had watched her actions from the time when she came upon these two Utopians until she spoiled their dreams and left Jimmie alone and full of the will to sabotage. But thru the opposite door which opened upon the old-fashioned passage way leading to the kitchen, two eyes had gazed upon her,—eyes of white and black and

fire. So Jimmie stood, holding his rag doll peril-
ously by the leg and trying to solve the mystery
of the sudden and terrible power which had interrupted the normal course of his life and carried
off his playmate, when Aunt Katy entered, chuckled,
took him into her arms, and with rather more
affection than she had lately bestowed upon him,
she hugged him to her bosom and carried him off
to the kitchen.

CHAPTER IV.

THE POWER OF CIRCUMSTANCE

No; environment is not omnipotent, but it is so almost all-powerful that it deserves the major consideration in the making of a man on earth. Here are two babies. Three-fourths of the blood of the one is from the same sources as three-fourths of the blood of the other. And that other fourth of blood is just—human blood. In physical feature they are like duplicates. But the divergence of their ways on earth will carry them to differing destinies.

And which is which? Why did Aunt Katy hug little William so passionately when alone with him? And when alone with little Jimmie, why did she croon so wierdly and almost compassionately over him, and treat him with all the indulgent pity of her race? William's aunt remarked the strange fascination with which Jimmie seemed to hold his grandmother.

And why had Aunt Katy done this thing which "Miss Ollie" feared would be done, and which the reader of this history must by this time suspect to have been done? Partly for fear and partly for revenge.

For fear: because she had often heard John Elliot tell, with approval, of the terrible vengeance wreaked by one of his brothers on "a little nigger gal." It seemed that the little colored girl was not much older than his brother's child whom she was supposed to nurse and take care of; and that by carelessness or childish neglect she had allowed the little white child to come too near a boiling pot in which soap was being made. The child stumbled, overturned the pot and scalded itself to death. The angry and brutal father then seized the little nurse and "cut both ears off that little nigger." All the other colored people had fled at the sight, so that "nobody ever knew what became of the rest of the little nigger gal," for not even the parents of the colored child had dared to address any inquiries to the infuriated demon who was responsible for her unrevealed fate. Aunt Katy recalled this oft repeated story and remembered that as John Elliot was leaving on the previous day, he had said to her concerning William: "Take good care of him,—for hell will be too good for any nigger if he gets hurt." And so, as the stove lid fell on that little leg, what was Aunt Katy to do when there was another pair of little legs just like them, close at hand and perfectly sound?

For revenge: because in the innermost of her soul she had always resented with deepest human

hate the outrage which John Elliot had committed
upon the innocence of her little Essie. Every slight
and every act of neglect or contempt which Essie
and Essie's child had suffered from the Elliots
and their kin, had deepened this hate and fed this
desire for revenge. Whenever John Elliot was the
offender, the inspiration to this deed had spoken in
her ear like a tempting devil.

So—well—when the Elliots returned from Eu-
rope, William had become quite fond of his New
Orleans aunt, but looked strangely upon his parents, which was "perfectly natural." He had to
be won over by his mother and father, but that was
soon done with a multitude of playthings and
goodies.

What did the babies care?

* * * * * *

We next see these two children when they are
seven years old. How swift is the passage of
childhood,—to the eye of the observer. But to the
child it seems longer, the longest period of life,—
like great oceans of time.

In outward appearances these two little boys had
become less alike, so that now there was no mis-
taking the one for the other. But if one disre-
garded the illusions and veneer of this world's for-
tunes and saw only their essential features, they
were still enough alike to be twins. Clothing and
the care of their bodies clearly distinguished them.
Besides, each had now a personality which could

never be confounded with the other. William was
generally well-dressed, well-shod, pampered and
autocratic. Essie's "little nigger Jim" was clad in
home-made things or cast-offs, and had a temper
to fight and a disposition to carry away the playthings of the little autocrat. The last named trait
was "proof of his sect," as the colloquialism used
by Mrs. Elliot would have it. She often pointed
to the differences between these two little spirits,
especially in the presence of John Elliot, in support of her theories about "blood,"—as if indeed
that was the only difference,—as if they were otherwise circumstanced alike,—when as a matter of
fact they were more nearly equally endowed with
"blood" than with any other thing.

But while William was an autocrat, Jimmie was
a revolutionist, a radical. Ever and anon was the
autocrat forced to call loudly for aid from the
greater powers against this unsubduable revolutionist. Aunt Katy, Essie and others of the servants had often to succor the titled possessor of
the throne. Some of these encounters were naturally provoked by the arrogance of the little
autocrat, who was beginning to overhear the conversations of his elders, and to understand that
between him and Jimmie there was some sort of
a gulf fixed,—a gulf which he himself might cross
and recross at will, but which forever shut Jimmie
out.

The Russo-Japanese war was going on, and

when a great naval battle was imminent, John Elliot had remarked to guests at table that the Jap-
anese could never win because they were "too much
like niggers." This unpremised conclusion about
"niggers" went unchallenged, as usual. William
had listened closely to this table-talk. And so in
the afternoon, when he carried his bean-shooting
cannon and his uniformed card-board soldiers into
the kitchen yard to play war with Jimmie, he
insisted that his side must be the "Rushins" and
and that Jimmie's side must be the "nigger Japs."
This was finally agreed to by Jimmie, as nationali-
ties were not so important to him. For Jimmie's
army consisted of soldiers of different sizes and
shapes and colors, which with the help of Aunt
Katy he had recruited with a pair of scissors from
old paper boxes, and a few faded, battered and
crippled, limbless or headless "Rushins" which the
opposing general magnanimously loaned him on
the eve of battle. And while Jimmie was setting
his motley army in battle array, it seems that the
"Rushin" general had the nerve to fire a shot at
them before the "nigger Jap" general "wuz ready
to give orders to shoot." In the heated parley
which followed from these oddly conflicting notions of the laws of war, the commanders came to
blows. And when John Elliot rushed from the
house with reinforcement for the distressed and
vociferous "Rushin," the opposing general had dis-
carded the conventional weapons of warfare, and

winding his left fingers in the curls of his antagonist, was pounding him with his right fist and
with the regularity of drumfire. At sight of this
savage attack, John Elliot, one of the great powers, rushed forward, seized the barbarian in the
back, gave him two hard spanks, then dropped him
and turned to console the rescued party. But instead of yielding tamely, the little Afro-Asiatic,
catching the great power for a moment off guard,
kicked him violently on the shin and retreated at
top speed. Whereupon that infuriated superman,
tho more insulted than injured, uttered this fear-
ful prophecy: "The little devil! that nigger will
die with his boots on."

Jimmie was now completely outlawed; all dip-
lomatic and commercial intercourse was forbidden,
and never again was he to be tolerated on the
premises of the Big House, the stronghold of the
powerful land-baron, John Elliot.

CHAPTER V.

THE TWO SCHOOLS

It is unnecessary to write the full story of the education and development of these two human beings. It would be but a history for which anyone who knows the conditions, might adduce a hundred parallels.

The little outlaw, Jimmie, was never again allowed on the Elliot premises. But whenever John Elliot saw Aunt Katy alone, he always inquired interestedly after "that little rascal." Elliot seldom saw Essie: with the intense partizanship and the sensitiveness of a mother, she had resented the exclusion of Jimmie and gradually grown away from personal service to the Elliots. She sought other work, washing, ironing and sewing at home. Meanwhile she married, unfortunately, one of the male minions of Elliot's household,—a tale-bearing Negro, one of those seemingly unnatural but ubiquitous products which spring up whenever one race presses another race down. This miserable wretch was continually filling Elliot's ear with evil reports, as to how: "Essie's spoilin' dat boy o'

her'n. I'se tried to be a step-daddy to him an'
make some'n out o' him. But Essie teaches him
to feel he jes' ez good ez any white boy, an' I
know ain't no good comin' uv a nigger whut grow
up thinkin' he good ez white fokes." Not only
was Jimmie thrust further and further away
from the possibility of any favor at the Big House,
but once Essie had to conceal the child for nearly
all winter to save him from the terrible wrath of
John Elliot, after Jimmie had thrashed Master William on the way home from their separate schools,
when their paths and their boyish wills happened
to cross.

These two children attended schools that were
not only separate but very different. William had
less than forty schoolmates, but two teachers, a
man and a woman, both college-trained people.
Jimmie had more than a hundred schoolmates, but
one teacher,—a man, who had probably gone to
school at sometime somewhere, but whose chief
qualification consisted of the fact that for years
he had helped John Elliot to recruit new "hands"
for the farm by inducing his illiterate and unwary
fellow-blacks in the Carolinas and Georgia to
"come west and make a fortune." William's
school opened in September and kept till May.
Jimmie's school was open for six or eight weeks in
the latter part of summer, after the crops were
"laid by," and again for six or eight weeks in the
dead of winter, between the end of the cotton-

picking season and the beginning of "breakin' ground" for spring planting. William sat in a schoolhouse that was fairly modern. Jimmie was taught in a colored church building, with scant light and board-shutter windows, which was rented by the schoolboard for one dollar a week.

*   *   *   *   *   *

A few years later William graduated from the high school in Little Rock, to which he had been sent after finishing the work of the local school. Jimmie, now grown to "Jim," had been taken out of school when he was in the "third reader," to help his unfortunate mother and his shiftless step-father to earn a living. The stepfather and John Elliot had agreed together that too much learning would spoil any "biggity yaller nigger."

These two boys, now eighteen years old, still resembled each other, but not as closely as when they were infants. Beings of the same genus or species are more alike in the earlier stages of their development. Up to a certain period in their growth the foetus of the human is even indistinguishable from that of the ape. Long since had the face of Jim ceased to be confounded in the mind of people with the face of William. But the colored people contended that Jim was much more "like the spit o' ole Man Elliot." Jim was angular and sunburned. William was rounded in feature and rather brunette, and the proud Mrs. Elliot said that he

bore the lines and complexion of her family, the
Prices, rather than those of the Elliots.

And now these two boys were about to enter
the two most important schools of their divergent
careers: William was to enter the State University, Jim was to enter the State Penitentiary.

"Father, what has been done about the case of
that nigger Jim?" inquired William, as he took
his last breakfast at home before leaving to catch
the train.

"Saved him from gettin' lynched—sendin' him
to pen' for four years—guess they'll teach him
somethin' there"—was the laconic reply.

"But, father, those boys told me that five of
them had Jim down, beating him, and that he
snatched a stick from one of them and knocked
the Brough boy's eye out while lying on his back
trying to beat the white boys off."

"Six niggers to one white man in this county,"
commented the senior Elliot,—"never do to let
one of 'em get away with a thing like that. But
if he hadn't been such a biggity nigger ——" and
Elliot looked far away as if dreaming, or remem
bering. "Never wanted to be treated like other
niggers, always in a fight. Essie's husband, Sam,
testified that Jim always led the nigger boys in
fights against white boys."

"I saw Essie yesterday, with her ten-year old
girl, Mary," said William, as his eyes moistened.
"They were very wretched; they certainly love

Jim. Somehow I felt very bad when I looked at them."

"At which one?" asked Elliot, as he bit savagely into his food. But just then his wife gave him a look which ended his remark.

"Both of them," said William, honestly, "but especially Essie. Her flushed face and pleading, suffering eyes made one feel sad."

John Elliot looked furtively at William, as he thought of Essie's beautiful little Mary. For the first time he felt a deep sense of guilt and accountability. For it matters not what we are, we always want our children to be the noblest.

After a few minutes of silence, William unwittingly showed where his unuttered thoughts had been, by continuing them aloud: "And they say that Jim's fight was about his little sister Mary. The Brough boy and his gang had shouted insults at her as she was going to school and ——."

"Well, my boy," interrupted Elliot, "you must be leaving to catch your train in two hours. Make sure that you have all your things packed. We expect you to make good in college. All we have is yours, as soon as you are ready to take charge of it. Your mother and I are gettin' old, you know."

"Speaking of Essie's eyes," put in Mrs. Elliot, who seemed to be unaware of Elliot's effort to change the subject of thought,—"speaking of eyes reminds me of the look which Jim gave me as

the sheriff was leading him away after his sentence. He frightened me, and it frightens me
every time I remember that look. I had really
never looked into his face since long ago, when
as a little boy he used to play around the house
here with you,"—and she directed her eyes at
William. And then, with that suddenness with
which some women can change from timid bird to
fierce feline, she looked reproachfully at John Elliot and continued: "But I just feel that no good
will ever come of the existence of that nigger,—
for nigger blood will tell."

The embarrassment was relieved by a confusion
and rushing of feet from the direction of the kitch-
en, and above it all the voice of Aunt Katy: "My
po' chile, my po' li'l chile! You must not suffer
so,—*you shall not suffer so!*" and Essie burst into
the Elliot dining room, her hair disheveled, her
face blotched with much weeping, and her left
arm around the beautiful neck of little Mary, who
clung to her mother and wept sympathetically.
Mary was of a shade between brown and yellow
and had very black and slightly wavy hair. And
as she stood clinging to the waist of the *mater
dolorosa*, the eye of the aritist might have seen
framed in that doorway a truer picture of innocence and beauty and of love and sorrow than in
a thousand madonnas.

Essie, her eyes suddenly flashing out of their
watery depths and blazing like pools of fire, spoke

with the effrontery and the unnatural temerity of madness: "John Eliot! John Eliot! My Jimmie,—he was just trying to save his little sister! You know what! God! You know what!"

Elliot bounded forward angrily, as if to shut off something which he feared was coming, but his right arm was seized by William, who said passionately: "Father! the poor thing is just crazy about her boy,—that is all. Let her go. Take her away, Aunt Katy."

Something seemed to stir in Mrs. Elliot, and for the first time in nearly twenty years she felt towards Essie as a real human and almost as a sister. She put her arms tremblingly about the sad, mad mother and said: "Poor girl, somehow I feel a great pity for Jim, too. Let us bear it, and perhaps all will be well."

The actions and sentimentality of his wife and his son had disarmed and almost unnerved John Elliot, and he strode impatiently and disgustedly out of the opposite door.

"Come, my po' li'l' chile," said Aunt Katy, gray-haired now, but erect, and with the same burning eyes,—"come, my baby," as she pulled along Essie, now unresisting,—"come home with yo' mammy an' she will console you," and shouting defiantly in the direction of the door out of which John Elliot had gone,—*"Yes, I can console her!"* And then the dry mirthless laugh of hysteria or secret vengeance, as she led her child and grandchild away.

Mrs. Elliot and William stood for a few moments unconscious of each other, and then she, as if waking from a dream, said: "Come, my boy, you must get ready for your train." And he, as if aroused from a trance: "O— er— yes, mother."

* * * * * *

When Mrs. Elliot was returning from seeing William off, she stopped her car when Essie hailed her by the side of the road: "Mis' Elliot, I hope I didn't hurt your feelin's," and she looked with such deep and genuine compassion upon the white mother that the latter was puzzled. "But we dearly love Jim," continued Essie, "an' we will always love him."

The somewhat mystified Mrs. Elliot ascribed this to madness and replied sympathetically, "And I will always pity him."

"An'—Mis' Elliot,—where is he gone?"

"Who?"

"My—er—Master William," said Essie, holding her breath.

"He has gone off to college for four years. The poor boy felt very sorry for you, Essie,—and for Jim."

And Mrs. Elliot drove on to the Big House.

CHAPTER VI.

THE TWO GRADUATES

William had spent his four years in college, and Jim his four in prison. John Elliot had told Aunt Katy that William was not to return to the plantation but would go direct from college to France, where he would live with his aunt, Madame Dupree, and study for a year or two. But Jim was coming home, and Aunt Katy and Essie, and Mary who was now nearly fifteen years old, were preparing to receive him. In spite of what Aunt Katy had told her, Essie still loved Jim,—and Aunt Katy loved him too. He was a part of their lives. Had he not been their boy from babyhood? And with all his waywardness, he had been affectionate and obedient to Aunt Katy and Essie, and to the beautiful little Mary he was big brother, worshipful knight and hero. Nearly all his fights and quarrels had been in defense of her. In the four years of his absence she had greatly idealized this devoted brother, for she did not share the secret of the older women. Essie loved Jim maternally, but she did not doubt the truth of the confession and

disclosure of Aunt Katy. And she remembered
that while they were in France and before they
left New York letters had come from the New
Orleans Aunt reciting how little "William" would
have nothing to do with her at first, and saying
that she had to gradually win him from the apron
strings of Aunt Katy in the kitchen. And the
thing was plain on its face,—when once you knew
it: for there was Jim, angular, pale, and tan,
phlegmatic and vindictive; while William was in
feature rounded and in color brunette, and sympathetic in disposition. But in spite of all, they
loved Jim, and were "killing the fattest calf," as
Aunt Katy expressed it, for his return.

There is no other mother heart on earth like
that which beats with African blood. It can love
the children of other mothers, even those of the
oppressor, almost as dearly as it loves its own.
The Negro mother is, not in mere fiction, but in
very fact of flesh and blood and affection, *the
greatest mother in the world*.

Jim met a royal welcome from these three.
Little Mary's father, Sam, was less cordial; he had
never liked Jim. When Jim was arrested for fight-
ing on account of Mary and for defending himself,
it was this tale-bearing step-father who had
sneaked around to the Big House: "Ah declare, Mr.
Ellyut, Ah allus wanted to do my dooty by Jim, but
he been de mos' onmannerl'est boy. Ah try to
teach him dat if he is a bright merlatter, he jes'

lak other niggers. But he ain't got no regards fer
me, an' Ah allus feared his hate 'g'inst white fokes
gwine git him in trouble." And in court he had
testified: "Ah nuvver could make dat boy mine me;
he wouldn't even go to Sunday school 'cause Ah
wuz de Soop'ntinder." And even this humorless
court had laughed.

But Aunt Katy and Essie welcomed Jim with
embraces and tears, while the self-conscious Mary
looked on with moist eyes. To her he had always
been a hero, and for the last four years she had
pictured him in her imagination as bravely endur-
ing some torture for the sake of his "Little Sis,"
as he called her. But the creature whom she now
saw in the arms of her mother and grandmother,
was so different from the creation of her dreams.
He was cold and hard and unsentimental. The welcome which had cost them all so much thought and
care and pains, did not seem to appeal to him. Indeed he spoke as if he did not expect to stay with
them but would go afar off. He showed tenderness only when he put his arms about Mary's
shoulders and patted her head, saying: "It was all
for you, Little Sis,." If there be any sentiment in
us, we will love those for whom we sacrifice and
for whom we suffer. We can love them even better than they can love us, for self-sacrifice is both
the cause and the effect of true love. Mother's
love is the greatest love in the world,—because
mother lays most upon the sacrificial altar.

They prevailed upon him to stay with them. Such
true and loving hearts could win even Jim. He
seldom talked in the presence of Sam, but when
alone with the other three, he would often describe bits of his experience and observations in
the awful state prison, telling of the rapacity and
brutality of the guards and keepers. He swore
violently whenever any one called the name of Elliot, so that Aunt Katy and Essie and Mary never
talked in his presence about the people at the Big
House. But Sam, who liked to talk about "de
white fokes," would occasionally mention, testing-
ly, "Mr. Ellyut;" whereupon Jim would utter an
oath and seize his hat and leave the cabin.

Jim never spoke to Elliot. Elliot never spoke to
Jim. The ex-convict managed to get a job with
a neighboring planter, as labor was scarce, and
one day as he was driving a wagon along the
roadside, he met Elliot on horseback. The road
was so narrow that even a man on horse could not
safely pass a wagon unless the latter drew a bit
to the side. Jim drove straight ahead in the middle
of the road, ignoring the approach of Elliot, so
that he had to turn his horse down a steep em-
bankment to escape the wagon. That evening Sam
kept eyeing Jim and hinting about work and wages,
and finally wound up: "I jes' happened by de Big
House. Our white fokes needs mo' han's, and dey
pays mor'n other white fokes, and Mr. Ellyut tol'
me to tell Jim ———."

"Go to hell!" said Jim, as he reached for his hat and walked out.

"Ah ain't been to no penitenchery," said Sam, "an' ain't had haff his opperchoonity to learn nuthin', but I got mo' manners dan dat nigger. He a wuss nigger dan he wuz fo' dey sent him off."

* * * * * *

Meanwhile Mrs. Elliot was receiving long letters from Madame Dupree, telling of William's arrival in Paris, of his studies and of the fine impression which he was making on the French people. When letters came from William, he invariably asked after Essie and her daughter and Aunt Katy, and often made inquiries about Jim. Mrs. Elliot was in the habit of reading these letters to Aunt Katy in the kitchen or dining room, because of the genuine interest which the latter manifested in any news from "Master William."

One day after reading one of these letters, the proud Mrs. Elliot commented: "I tell you, Aunt Katy, altho nigger boys don't have the same privilege as white boys, still if they had any ambition to learn and work and do what they *can* do, they might make *their* mothers happy instead of causing them so much trouble. " Aunt Katy's reply was a speechless gaze, which would have been eloquent, had Mrs. Elliot been the wiser. If only white people could read the minds of black people ———. But one day Aunt Katy's patience suddenly gave way under the unconscious attack which the white woman was continually making on the black grandmother's secret knowledge and firm convictions: "Mis' Elliot, I don't b'lieve any mo' in this blood business. If Jim had had the other chile's *chance*,—who knows? I heard you read one day from Master William's letter that there was some colored boys over there from Georgia an' South C'lina, an' that they done as well as anybody in their studies. Perhaps those white people over there act different toward colored people and give 'em a better chance. Essie says the for'n white folks in Paris treated her nicer'n her own white folks treated her, an' ————."

"Katy!" shouted Mrs. Elliot, dropping the saving grace of "Aunt," while her face reddened and almost bursted, "at your age and with the training you have had, you ought to know better. If God had meant for your race to be like white people, he would not have made you black! And I'll bet those niggers that William spoke of, are almost white and have a lot of white blood ————."

"*Lot o' white blood!*" shrieked Aunt Katy,—"an' so has Jim! He is certainly white, *al-most.*"

Her eyes blazed,—she was beside herself,—she was struggling against some inner urge to disclose some awful history or utter some terrifying prophecy. Her very audacity amazed Mrs. Elliot, who stood paralyzed by anger and wounded pride. Her mind was struggling against the impossible task of conceiving some adequate rebuke when Mary burst in upon them: "O Aunt Katy!"—as she called her own grandmother,—"O Mis' Elliot! They are after him again,—bloodhounds,—guns!"

Seizing the hand of the excited girl, Aunt Katy made off for the cabin and Essie. As she rushed out, she laughed the uncanny laugh and said: "Vengeance of God!"

As the yelp of dogs and a few scattered shots were heard, Mrs. Elliot mechanically paraphrased: *"The vengeance of the gods!"*

CHAPTER VII.

THE COAT AND THE HAT

"The coat and hat were found in the cabin of that nigger Jim," said the one-eyed Brough, "and that proves he's the criminal."

"But the coat and hat are not his," suggested John Elliot, diplomatically; "they are known to be the property of some white man."

"Makes no diff'rence," snorted Brough, the mob leader, "he's the nigger, and his name is hash this time. He can't escape; we've hemmed him in the swamp. Not even his sympathizing kin will be able to save his neck this time."

John Elliot was not to be thus insulted, not even by another white man. He reached for his gun: "Say that I am right in what I think you mean, and, damn you! I'll shoot you like a dog, you po' white devil!"

"O, I mean Essie," the dodging coward quickly replied, "she's trying her best to lie him out of this."

"Yes," said John Elliot, compromised by this cowardice of Brough, altho he knew that the in-

sinuation did not refer to Essie. But with all the
easy presumptousness of the landowner class, he
continued: "And now you are going to shut your
mouth and hear *me* tell just what she does say
about it. Then you and these gentlemen," diplomatically, "may do as you damn please. Essie's
a nigger, but her story agrees in the main points
with that of the white woman. The white woman
says that the man who stopped her buggy and assaulted her, was white; and that when he put her
back into the buggy and ordered her to drive on,
she heard another vehicle approaching from the
cross-road; and that later she saw her assailant
going across a field, as if frightened away without
his coat and hat. Now Essie says that Jim was
driving that way and picked up a coat and hat,
which he brought home."

To relieve the situation an older member of the
mob now spoke up in Brough's stead: "I don't
mean to make any insinuations or insulting re-
marks at all, Mr. Elliot, but I'm used to consistent lying on the part of niggers. The uppish kind
always help each other,—and she's his mother,
and blood is thicker'n water." And John Elliot
winced. "The lady did say that the man was
white, but ain't Jim white?" And as the speaker
noticed John Elliot's gun-hand creeping, he added
exegetically: "I mean, ain't he a *light nigger* who
could be mistaken for a white man in the dark?
And yo' own darkey Sam says Jim acted suspici-

ous when he brought the coat and hat in, and soon
as Sam knew a coat and hat figgered in the case,
he came and told us."

"Come here, Sam!" shouted a third member of
the mob,—"here, nigger, come and tell Mr. Elliot
jus' what you tol' us."

That frightened wretch came forth, or rather was
thrust forward from the center of the mob, which,
as a reward for his miserable lies, had held him
like a hostage and treated him almost as if he were
the criminal himself. They had hinted again and
again in his hearing that, if they did not catch Jim,
they might try their guns on "the first nigger they
could get their hands on."

Sam's statement, therefore, was more a plea for
his own hide than for any other purpose: "Ah
knowed it wuz Jim,—he ain't my chile, you see"—
and when he noticed Elliot's eyes batting fast, he
explained: "Ah mean, he's jes' only Essie's chile.
An' jes' ez soon ez Ah hyeahs 'bout de trouble, Ah
sez ter myself, sez Ah: 'Sam ain't gwine ter git
into no trouble 'bout dis boy.' 'Cause Ah done tried
ter make him behave lak a good nigger, ever since
Ah married his mammy. You see, he ain't my chile,
—jes' only Essie's chile by herse'f erlone, Ah mean,
—an' it ain't my fault, white fokes, dat he ain't
raised right, an' ——"

"Hurry up, nigger!" shouted two or three im-
patient men.

"Soon ez Ah hyeahd dat a lady wuz 'sa'lted and

dat de white gen'mens wuz lookin' fer de coat an' hat, Ah went straight an' tol' de white fokes. An' Ah tol' his mammy atterwards, an' she done tol' Jim. An' she sez he 'splain ter her dat he ain't done it, but she tell him ter run 'fo' de white fokes come. But Mr. Ellyut kin bear me witness dat I didn't marry her 'till long atter Jim wuz borned, an' ————."

"Shut up, nigger,—come on!" And the mob dragged him away frightened almost unto death for his life. Mr. Elliot stood silent. But was he convinced or compromised?

CHAPTER VIII.

THE MAN HUNT

Who can describe its fascination, and the madness? Hunting wild beasts is not to be compared with the hunting of a man. And once indulged in, it is seductive, like drinking alcohol or eating human flesh. There is more uncertainty and consequently more of the spirit of gamble in the man-hunt. The beast you can figure out too easily; you can tell just what he will do under a given set of circumstances. It is more a matter of science, and the sensuous animal is but part of your experimental material. But a man,—even a poor, oppressed and imbruted devil of a man,—has a wit like yours. It is not so easy to figure him out, for he is also figuring you out. He may, and he may not. His psychology is not a mere calculable thing; it is a thing that also calculates. You have to play more of a game against the man. It is thought against thought, scheme against scheme. Hunger and thirst do not drive him from his refuge as readily as it drives a beast from his lair. You must think and guess and doubt, rather than plan and calculate and feel sure. And paradoxically enough, some strategems can be used against the man which are useless against the brute: for the man has reason and faith, ambition and sentiment. A camouflage, a threat against his mother or a word from his sweetheart might fool or rouse or tempt the man. Sentiment might betray the human, where rigid instinct protects the animal.

Colored men who were friends or acquaintances of Jim, were compelled to go thru the swamp at night, followed closely by armed white men. These Negroes were ordered to engage in conversation, in which they had been drilled beforehand, and which was calculated to betray the fugitive:

"Dem white fokes done got tired huntin' Jim," in a loud voice.

"Ya-as, dey ain't doin' much night watchin' now, —didn't see none uv 'em where we entered de swamp."

"Uh-huh! If we could only run across Jim now, we could help him out, couldn't we?"

"A'nt Katy done tol' me dis mawnin' dat she got a hunderd dollars fer him to run off North wid, if she kin git it to him."

Letters were also dropped in different parts of the swamp and neighboring woods, purporting to be from Aunt Katy or Essie or other colored people, telling Jim just when and where he might get food and how he might escape. Once a report was spread around that Jim's mother, Essie, was very sick, and that Mary was dying. At another time word was passed around that Jim was not the right man after all, but that the right man had been caught and lodged in jail.

The mob members, with all their cunning, were making two fundamental mistakes: first, they were using colored people, against their will, as the agents and the medium of all these lies and attempted decoys; and second, they were at the same time abusing, bullying and maltreating innocent colored people, so that no Negro could possibly sympathize with the mob. It should have been expected that under such conditions these people, with their wonderful intuition, would use all their cunning to foil the pursuers.

One day Sam was informed by the mob that he would be sent into the swamp at night to find Jim. "O Lawdy Gawd, white fokes, dat nigger'll kill me!"

"Well, he's yo' son, ain't he?" suggested Brough, with a general "haw-haw!"

The idea might have been at first a jest, but the instant and sincere terror of Sam was so delicious to his tormentors, that when night came they made good the jest and actually started Sam toward the swamp at the points of their guns. Breaking under the torture, he shrieked aloud, foamed at the mouth and tore at his own flesh. He was mad. They shot him like a dog.

But if we fail to seduce a people or destroy a man thru their vices, we may still attack them thru their virtues. The devil sometimes assails a man via his strong points and makes his virtue his misfortune. So the man-hunters began to think: Perhaps these colored people are "traitors;" perhaps they are in touch with Jim; they may be warning him against our traps; possibly these colored people are doing for this colored man exactly what under similar circumstances we white people would do for any white man,—give him warning and aid. There now, we have it: *We must also fool these people;* they must be made to lead Jim into a trap without knowing themselves that it is a trap.

That is, they would betray these people and this fugitive thru their virtues. The colored people are strong in sympathy, and when once they feel deeply, in loyalty; and Jim was strong in physical courage and in self-sacrificing love for Essie and Mary. "That's it," said one of the mob, "we'll get him thru his womenfolks. We'll let the niggers know that we're fixing to give the two wenches hell tomorrow night, an' they'll be sure to slip the word along to Jim. He's got a lot o' nerve, and that'll get him out."

"Yes, he always would fight for the gal," testified the one-eyed Brough.

So the plot was laid. The mob, still calling itself a *posse* and assuming all law, issued a decree that Essie and her daughter should stay in the cabin all the next day and night and that no colored person was to go there under pain of chastisement by the posse.

This had the desired effect: it aroused the sincere curiosity of the colored people. What was going to be done to these defenseless women? Negroes working around white people became all eyes and ears. And members of the mob easily managed to let their servants overhear bits of the plan: "They're good-lookin' wenches an' the boys are goin' to call on 'em tomorrow night,—a dozen or so of the young fellows. Brough'll be with 'em,—he ain't never forgot how he lost his eye."

"Haw! haw! An' he wants more'n an eye for his eye, don't he?"

"An' after that the boys are going to burn the cabin down."

"After that they won't be fit for nothin' *but* burnin'." Some exaggerations were thrown in to fire the imagination of the colored people.

The simple-minded, sympathetic black folk were horrified. Calculations did not go amiss as to their sentiment and endeavors now. They slipped the news to Jim by way of "the grape vine telegraph," even while the posse kept closer watch on the swamp. For Jim was not in the swamp; his colored friends had got him out of the swamp the next day after he went into it. For many days he had been hidden in Elliot's great barn and was being fed from the kitchen of the Big House,—without the knowledge of the Elliots, however.

The character and courage of Jim also justified
the compliment which his enemies had paid him;
for when he heard that danger threatened Essie,
and his "Little Sis'" for whom he had already
sacrificed his life, he resolved not to be kept away
from them by consideration of life or death or hell.
He believed that the mob meant to carry out the
diabolical plot against those whom he loved, because the colored people who reported it to him
believed it. People who believe what they say,
have a way of making others believe. But the
colored people believed it only because the whites
apparently had tried to keep them from getting
wind of it. Jim resolved therefore to rescue Essie
and Mary or die. He was watching for a chance.
He would wait till dusk of evening. If by that
time he was given no chance, he would take one.

What was it that brought John Elliot wandering thru the great barn that afternoon? Are there
unseen powers that sport with our destinies as we
manipulate the lives of lesser creatures? The barn
was nearly half a mile from the Big House. Had
the actions of some servant made Elliot suspicious,
or was his troubled and wandering mind leading
him? Was there some soul-liaison, unrecognized
by both of them, between this old man and that
son of his hidden in the hay loft? At any rate,
there came Elliot in his wide hat, long coat and
gray trousers. From his lair in the loft Jim could
see him. The fugitive's mind worked fast: That

hat, coat, trousers,—they would be passports.—The
hunted man is more dangerous than the hunted
animal.—But was Elliot armed, as usual? Jim
evolved a plan. He climbed rapidly down and
walked out of the barn right before the astonished
eyes of Elliot.

"Stop!" demanded Elliot, reaching for his hip-
pocket. But Jim had passed out of the door. He
did not attempt to run but stepped behind the great
tree that stood in the barnyard on the side farthest
from the Big House. This looked pacific to John
Elliot, so he did not draw his gun: "Now, Jim,
you've got to surrender."

"Surrender hell!" said Jim, to Elliot's great ir-
ritation. And he let his pursuer see him reach out
from behind the tree and seize a huge billet of
wood. This angered Elliot. Jim meant to anger
him. To enrage a man is often the first step toward overcoming him.

Out flashed the ubiquitous Southern gun: "What
are you going to do with that club, nigger?"

"I may kill you with it,—you white devil!" hissed
the fugitive.

How the hot blood surged to Elliot's head. No
Negro ever said as much to a white man and lived,
—at least not within the borders of Arkansas and
the memory of John Elliot. He was too angry
to reply to this threat and insult. He simply began to move around the tree brandishing his gun
and trying to get a good aim at the object of his

wrath. This was the battle which Jim wanted to
provoke. He stuck close to the tree, while Elliot
moved around at a distance but did not risk coming
closer. The younger man moved easily in the
smaller circle; the raging old man found it more
difficult to keep pace in the larger circle. How
exasperating it is for one whom we consider inferior to first defy us and then to outwit us. Finally in a blind rage John Elliot fired two shots,
cutting the bark of the tree on his right and at
Jim's left, as the two men facing each other moved
in their orbits from right to left.

These shots were a signal to the quick-witted
fugitive. He was waiting for some such sign. It
indicated that his pursuer had become desperate,
and therefore indiscrete and less clear in judgment.
John Elliot had the gun, but cunning is the weapon
of the weak and of the unarmed. This was the
moment for the ruse: he hung his hat on the end
of his club, holding it in his left, so that Elliot
might see only the crown of the hat Another
shot rang out, a piece flew from the crown of the
hat, and Jim fell backward to the ground, slapping
the hat quickly on his head. He pressed his palm
over the rift in its crown and closed his eyes as
if in great pain. Elliot rushed forward: "It was
your own fault: I didn't want to shoot you." And
as he stooped to pull Jim's hand from the top of
his head, the prostrate man with the irresistible-
ness of the unexpected suddenly jerked both of

Elliot's legs from under him; and as the latter
fell, the gun flew from his hand. The greater
agility of the younger man brought him first to
his feet and he got possession of the gun. He
ordered Elliot to go immediately into the barn.
Outwitted but haughty, Elliot refused to utter a
word, but he obeyed the command, for there was
a light in Jim's eye which no rational creature
would disregard.

Inside the barn, Jim for the first time in his life
said to this proud baron what both of them thought
to be the truth: "John Elliot, I am your bastard
son. That is the only reason why I am not goin'
to kill you. It is not because I think you deserve
to live nor that I fear to die. If I were not your
son, I would kill you for your treatment of my
mother. But if any harm comes to her now, or
to my sister I *will* kill you in broad daylight if
necessary, even at the door of the jail or at the
gate of hell,—your own son with your own gun.
For the present I only want your clothes,—hat,
coat and pants. Take 'em off. You can put on
these,--if you want to."

Elliot, proudly silent, gave up his own clothes,
but appeared not to see the coat which Jim held
out to him.

"And now I'll tie you up in the loft, so you can't
get loose, but you can call for help later. I will
tell you when to call, and don't call too soon or
you won't get the help. You are to stay here all

night. I have staid here many nights. Do **not**
call or notify any of the boys when they feed **and**
put up this evenin'. I will be watchin', and **if I**
see the least sign that they have found you I **will**
come out and kill you right before their faces. **I**
ain't anxious to escape and I ain't hankerin' **to**
live. I'm tryin' my best to get my mammy **and**
Little Sis' away from here tonight; and if we **get**
away all right, it may save you some trouble."

* * * * * *

That evening after sundown but before **dark,**
when his colored peons were putting up their **mules**
and feeding and milking, Elliot could overhear
them discussing the man-hunt and Jim and himself. He was amazed at the accurateness of **the**
knowledge of these semi-slaves and reddened unseen at some of the compliments he heard paid **to**
himself. But he uttered not a word and scarcely
dared to breathe, lest he innocently betray his involuntary hiding place; for he knew that death,
fearless death, had his eye on him.

Night came on, and as her husband was not **at**
home by eleven o'clock, Mrs. Elliot phoned **an**
inquiry to the plantation storekeeper at the **little**
village square. She was informed that her husband had driven up in front of the store in **the**
earlier part of the night; that he did not get **out**
but ordered certain provisions brought out to **his**
car, and told the clerk to tell Mrs. Elliot, if **she**
inquired, that he was driving to Augusta, **twelve**

or fifteen miles away, and might possibly not return till morning. The clerk remarked that there
were several other people in the back of the auto-
mobile.

Why had he not told her himself and earlier?
The wife had forebodings. "Where is Aunt Katy?"
"She went to see Essie and Mary, ma'm, d'rectly
after supper." Yes, Mrs. Elliot remembered hearing her vow that she would spend the next two
nights in the cabin with her "chillun, and see if
any po' white trash dared to touch 'em."

Mrs. Elliot retired and dreamed disturbing
dreams: William was a little boy again. He had
fallen into a deep well. Aunt Katy and Essie were
doing their best to rescue him with a long rope;
but every time they got him near the top of the
well, some white person of a crowd who stood
near, would cut the rope so that William would
drop back, and the shortened rope would make it
more difficult for the struggling women to reach
him next time. Somehow, as is the horror of
dreams, the dreamer seemed spellbound against
rendering aid and dumb to protest, when finally
the likeness of John Elliot rushed up to lend a
hand for the rescue, and suddenly and as if against
his will a knife appeared in his hand and he himself cut the rope short from the hands of the despairing women. And the dreamer was struggling
against her dumbness and numbness for freedom
to move or shriek, when ———

"'Scuse me, Mis' Ellyut, fer wakin' yo' so early," a servant was saying with the best effort at the English, "but Mr. Brough is hyeah, an' he sez he jes' *hafter* speak ter yo' at oncet."

What was wrong? Brough? A bad omen in all this trouble for years. She hurried to dress partially, and went to the sitting room where she was confronted by the one-eyed mob-leader and two other hard-looking men.

"Pardon, Madam," one of them began as they observed her honestly puzzled mien, "but we wonder if you can tell us where Mr. Elliot has gone and what he has gone for."

This wounded her pride more than was intended, for in very truth she did not know. She parried: "And pray what is that to you?" as she eyed Brough haughtily and suspiciously.

"Well, Madam, to be plain and brief," retorted that worthy, "we've just driven to Augusta to make sure, and we find that he or somebody just like him left on the ten-thirty train for Missouri by the Iron Mountain Railroad,—and what's more," he now spoke maliciously and with curling lips, "he carried the old nigger woman and Essie and the other little wench with him. Did you know they were gone?"

This was a moment of trial for Mrs. Elliot. The ring of triumph in Brough's voice annoyed her. But it also aroused her Bourbon blood which resents the encroachments of "po' white trash" even more than the familiarity of "niggers." She deliberately accepted the challenge with the simple reply: *"It's a lie!"*

But when a rude man has the advantage which Brough thought he had, he can afford to be generous, which he translates into being more deliberately and more successfully cruel. So rudely ignoring her contempt and disregarding her excitement, he coolly continued: "When I heard he was driving to town with female parties in his car, *I* got suspicious. I sent my nigger to the cabin and nobody answered when he knocked. Then we went there after midnight and broke in. The wenches were not there, and some of your other niggers told us the old woman was not at the Big House and that Elliot was not at home. We drove as fast as we could to Augusta to investigate and ———."

"O Mis' Ellyut, Marse Ellyut sez sen' him some clo'es to the big barn quick, an' he done tol' me to tell yo' he'll be hyeah right away!"

The proud matron now looked upon the three confused men with the anger of a tigress. No words accompanied that look. No words were adequate to accompany it. Her scorn was ineffable,— but mingled with amazement, doubt and fear. Commanding the excited servant to follow her, she hurried into a room and returned with a suit of Elliot's clothes. Brough and his men followed her hurried footsteps to the barn, where they remained outside with the others while she went in to find Elliot.

When the landlord emerged from his humiliating confinement, his anger was consuming: "The damned brute caught me here at about three in the afternoon. Tied me in the loft. Took my clothes. Left his rags and ran off." He added some words of fire but did not give the other details of the evening's transactions.

"That explains all," said Brough quickly. "He and the nigger women are on their way North. We must wire the governor and have them headed off."

"They stole my car," said Elliot, who had been tlaking with Mrs. Elliot, "they all ought to be sent to jail, and that dangerous nigger Jim should be lynched!"

"Right—O!" shouted Brough.

And the man-hunt became statewide and almost national.

CHAPTER IX.

THE TATTOO AND THE SCAR

What a wonderful thing is organization when inspired by a feeling of racial solidarity. No white man save his immediate oppressors seemed interested in Jim, the peon. But Jim, the "bad nigger," the fugitive, the alleged rapist, attracted the attention of the governments of half a dozen neighboring states and of the whole white world thru the associated press. Who can calculate the value of the money and the time spent in efforts to apprehend this "criminal?" And who can refrain from speculating as to how much more good even the one hundredth part of that money and time and attention might have accomplished, had they been bestowed on the education and training of this human being thru his childhood and youth? Within a few hours the great press had made this unfortunate and unknown creature notorious. A special representative of the Little Rock newspapers had visited the scene and published thrilling myths of this almost superhuman demon, "a very light-skinned Negro." Not a single word, however, was offered in explanation of his *lightness* of skin. The papers naturally got things a bit mixed up, and told how "Jim," a mongrel creature with no surname, had betrayed the confidence of his employer, John Elliot, a prominent white planter; had criminally assaulted this planter's little daughter; and that the child was hardly expected to live. Then he was credited with having attempted to foment a general uprising among the blacks and overthrow the government of white people and force upon them "social equality" and other horrors. Failing in this because of the courage and generalship of one "Colonel" Brough, he had then attempted to abduct the wealthy planter, John Elliot, as a hostage; and had held him a prisoner for several days until the insurrectionist was forced to retreat by a sudden onslaught from Brough; whereupon he fled in stolen "automobiles," compelling a few blacks at the point of his gun to follow him. One far-away Northern editor, innocently reflecting all these lies and fictions, said that "this hybrid, who is perhaps Caucasian and Indian rather than Negro, is the Villa of Arkansas."

The governor of Missouri had dispatched officers to Poplar Bluff to search every train and take this outlaw, dead or alive. But the governor of Arkansas had trains stopped and searched at Hoxie before they entered Missouri. In their haste and excitement orders had been issued from Little Rock only for the arrest of Jim, "a very bright mulatto with Anglo-Saxon features, intelligent, probably passing for white." But when Aunt Katy saw them overpowering Jim, she joined promptly in the fight and was also seized and held by the officers. The lively fight put up by Jim and Aunt Katy attracted all attention to themselves, so that Essie and Mary were unnoticed. In the confusion they were left on the train and escaped into Missouri.

The captives were hurried back to the place from which they had escaped. What a gala day in all that country side when the news spread: "They caught him!" What glad tidings: "They got that nigger!" It was the merry greeting of every little white school child: "Gee! won't they lynch him tho?" Nobody seemed to have the remotest idea of courts, trials and convictions. It was like as if a wild beast, dangerous to the whole community, had been trapped, and everybody was to go now and witness its slaughter and rejoice.

When Jim and Aunt Katy were brought back to the little village or business center of the plantations, bells were rung, guns were fired, and everybody, even the colored people, turned out as a matter of course to see. Returning heroes crowned with the laurel of victory could not have attracted more attention. But these were lodged in jail. There seemed to be perfect harmony and goodwill between the officers of the law and the people. A certain spirit of preparation was in the air. People ate their suppers hurriedly, if they ate at all. Yes, they were to witness the biggest event in the history of that village,—a double lynching,—and "both a nigger man and a nigger wench."   Poor old Aunt Katy, to whose age the last few days had seemed to add as many years, had grown equally as much in fame.   Rumor had made of her a great sorceress and really the arch-fiend in the whole deviltry,—whatever it was.   For most of the gathering mob could not tell just what the crime was.   Of course murder and rape and "little white girls" were mixed up in it; but just who, when, how many and how much, nobody had clearly in mind.   But a conviction and a determination possessed all minds, and doubt would have been insanity.

And most of these people, nearly all of them, did not feel that anything wrong was about to be done, but something gloriously right or vindicatory, almost religious and sacred.   Generations before, men had not felt that anything was going wrong in New England when they burned wrinkled old women for witches.   Those who were not to be the performers or participants, were to be the audience or the "fans," as at ball games or bull fights.   The relative merits of hanging or shooting or burning were freely discussed.   Finally a compromise plan was hit upon; they were to be taken out to the back of Elliot's barn, to the tree where Jim, as rumor now ran, had done his best to "murder old man Elliot."   There they were to be hung and shot; and then they would be dragged

back to the village square and burned. This pro-
gram would satisfy all reasonable tastes.—A huge
pile of boards, boxes, pine knots, and straw was in
evidence before nightfall.

* * * * * *

Meanwhile what other fates were at work among
what other people in what other parts of the
world? William Elliot was doing service in the
French army and had requested his aunt, Madame
Dupree, to read all his mail from America before
sending it to him. This was partly a precaution
because his mother often sent messages in letters
to him for her sister, and also because he hoped
that his aunt might save him much time by reply-
ing immediately to some of these letters. And so
it happened that comfortably seating herself in
the boudoir of her Paris home, Madame opened
and read the following letter, stirring and moving
herself occasionally to see if she were really
awake:

"Dere master William, i no you will fergive yo
own mammy, an i you because i am a por mizzer-
able creetur, an has nobody in this worl but Essie
an you, an Jim. An the one you thinks you be-
long to, aint yo ma. She red all yo letters to me
an i no ther aint no coller line no race hate in
france, an if you no the truth you wood hep yo
own mammy an granny out from here, you not
miss Elliotts babie i done it mysef. i can explaine

to you Jim is hern. You wuz put in his place when you wuz to little babes. yo sister Mary do not no. i rite mysef, she direct envellup for me. you lernd nouff in that free cuntry to no collor don't count an you wont mine heppin yo own mammy an me an yo sister Mary. The burnt chile wuz hern mis Elliotts. i can prove, if you sen for us.

"Essie nose; i jes tole her. but she wont rite for fere hurtin you. She dont no i rite. you sen letter in my name.

"yo own granma,
"KATY PORTER."

With the swiftness of those who are fired with desperate purpose, Madame Dupree made plans at once to visit America and her sisters. Monsieur Dupree had often suggested that she do so; and now for fear that she might change her mind he refrained from expressing surprise or asking any questions about her sudden decision.

She would sail tomorrow. She was afire—she wanted to telegraph William,—but no,—was it true? And then she remembered how dark he seemed, and—what she had been praising in him as a handsome roundness of feature. Could it be true? What had the other child become? He must be a man as old as William. What good would it do to prove this wretched thing? Should she not drop it? It made no difference—in France.—She remembered that she had never spoken to William about that tattoo,—had never heard him speak of it. Her mind ran repeatedly thru all the events of her visit with the Elliot's over twenty years ago.

With all this tumult in her soul she sailed out upon the tumultuous Atlantic. And then alone with the great lonesomeness of being one among many strangers, and like an atom on the inhospitable and interminable ocean, she became still more introspective and doubtful of the wisdom of her way: Should she not have seen William? Should she not have asked the advice of Mr. Dupree? The French people seem so cool and sensible about such things.—Should she not have sent the letter to her sister? Or to her New Orleans sister and gotten her viewpoint? Should she not have destroyed the letter altogether and then written Aunt Katy a threat in her own name,— or a complete rejection and signed the name of William to it? That might have stopped Aunt Katy from ever writing again.—Perhaps she might still do something like that. But how could she ever explain her sudden coming? And how could she ever keep such a secret anyway?—O, the fascination with which fate draws us on—to see and to know fully. The victim tends to ensnare himself. The criminal tends to become his own betrayer, his own judge, and sometimes his own executioner.

There is humor in fate; and irony and sarcasm. When she reached Augusta, she engaged a man to drive her out to "Elliot's Place." This man having agreed to do so for a very moderate fee, noticed her surprise and explained: "O, me an' some o' the boys wuz goin' aout anyhaow this evenin'—some niggers air to be lynched out thare to-night." To this she made no reply; it made her feel faint; she remembered Paris and civilization: the contrast was humiliating. She mused: "Can it be, O, can it be that my own nephew, my real nephew is a member of a group that can be—lynched?"

The Elliots had been silent during the awful preparations of that day. Silence does not always mean consent; it is sometimes the expression of unwilling acquiescence, or helplessness, or fear. The better South has been almost absolutely silent during half a century of lynch law,—and even now is but barely audible.—When Jim and Aunt Katy were led by the mob to the tree back of Elliot's barn, he went out apparently to protest, tho he knew the futlity of protest at this stage of the proceedings. The causes of this present storm had been operating for days and weeks and years. The seed of long ago had now become a fruit.

After he had gone out, Madame Dupree came in. She found Mrs. Elliot alone, pale and haggard, and staring wildly from the easy chair in which

she sat and from which she seemed unable to rise.
She had been prostrated by the terrible events of
the day, and altho her sister had wired from New
York and phoned hastily from Augusta, she was
yet puzzled by the suddenness and the coincidences
of this visit. "O, my good sister, you have come.
It is horrrible; I always said no good would come
of it, and now Jim and Aunt Katy————"

Madame Dupree, because of what was in her own
mind, anticipated and misinterpreted the allusions
of her sister and interrupted: "Then you know
about it? Then it is true?"

Mrs. Elliott, still busy with her own thoughts,
continued: "Have they told you? O, it is terrible!
It will spoil your visit; I am sorry you came into
it."

Madame Dupree fell limp into a great chair, and
to relieve herself and her sister of the pain of
further speech, she handed Mrs. Elliott Aunt Katy's
letter, to show the source and the extent of her
knowledge of the case, and the cause of her unexpected visit to America.

What pen can describe the infinite agony of that
minute? The stricken mother jumped to her feet
with the stare of madness in her eyes: "O God
of Vengeance! I mean they are lynching him
now—Jim--William!"

Shots and yells rang out, as if to punctuate this
terrible announcement and interpret it to the bewildered mind of Madame Dupree. Mrs. Elliot

bounded thru the door like a bereaved mother lioness, and her sister followed. When they reached the edge of the mob, they could see dangling under the tree a few feet from the ground what had been a human body and was now a mass of torn flesh and tattered clothes. Buckshot and rifle ball had rioted thru this human form.

And there was Aunt Katy standing with her back to the tree near the body, and holding the crowd at bay with a double-barreled shot gun which she had evidently managed to seize during the excitement attending the shooting of Jim. "I told you to keep the old witch tied!" said a voice.—With a fierce look of the African jungle, more feline than human, and with a coolness which for the moment commanded universal regard, she was saying in her dialect: "I do not want to kill. I do not want to live. I mean to tell John Elliot: *His own son has been killed!*"

"We know that," put in Brough.

"I mean Mis' Elliot's son. I can prove it. I want to prove it to John Elliot and die! *She* did not know but I knew that her child had a blue mark under its arm. This is her child. Look and see. William in France is Essie's child. I changed them when yo' child got burned, when you went off to France. Ha! ha! ha!" And in the light of torch and lantern she pointed an inexorable finger at John Elliot.

The mob stood silent for a moment, as if under

the spell of a real witch. A voice broke the spell: "It's a damned lie!" It was the voice of John Elliot. The mob, as if released from the spell by the magic of this oath, was about to make a desperate move on Aunt Katy, when a female voice put in: "I can tell. I am William's aunt from France. I tattooed his arm when he was an infant."

Ignoring Aunt Katy for the moment, Brough, the mob leader, took a lantern and led the newcomer to the dangling figure. Trembling, she lifted the mutilated arm, pushed up the remnant of a blood soaked sleeve, and fell fainting as she said: "The tattoo! It—is—*true!*"

This sudden turn of affairs killed the enthusiasm of the mob. And while attention was diverted from her, Aunt Katy slipped away, and a heavy plunge was heard in the great cistern that stood near.

Mrs. Elliot never regained her reason. "Vengeance of the Gods!" is her only coherent utterance.

John Elliot is opposed to lynching, and has spoken sentiments concerning miscegenation, interracial bastardy and "social equality," which make him somewhat unpopular in Arkansas.

The boy in France, so it is rumored, has been given a liberal portion of the Elliot money.

When Essie and Mary reached St. Louis, they were arrested and their extradition was demanded of the executive of that state. A great national organization of colored people and liberal-minded whites immediately began a legal battle to prevent the return of these women to Arkansas. Their case, however, was seemingly hopeless, as the governor of Arkansas had pledged "protection and a fair trial," when suddenly the governor of Missouri announced that extradition was denied. Those close to the governor say that he received a letter from the great Arkansas planter who seemed to be the center of the trouble and whose name had been prominent in all dispatches, and that this letter said that it was all a mistake to charge the two women with any connection with the crimes, that they were innocent, and that they could not secure justice and might be mobbed if they were sent back.—They are living in France with William Elliot, a captain in the French Army.

Aunt Katy was never removed from the grave she had chosen. The cistern was filled up with rocks and soil, and the resultant crater is known to-day as "Witch's Hole" where a great "conjure woman" or sorceress is said to have disappeared.

THE SUPERIOR RACE

Why is it that Jefferson D. Jones, Professor of Anthropology in the Mobile Institute, is now so singularly silent or noncommittal whenever the inherent inferiority of the Negro is being discussed in the various clubs of which he is a member, or at the social functions where he is a guest? Previously he has always taken the lead in these discusions. Indeed he had a hundred times demonstrated, anthropologically, that the Negro is not only inferior but must forever remain so, "showing conclusively," as a local editor said, "that altho the theory of evolution may prove that the white man, the nigger, the monkey and other mammalians sprung from some common origin, still the white man is the only one who has a soul, because the white man keeps on developing, while the monkey and the nigger have run into a sort of evolutionary cul-de-sac." A Chicago magazine had also published from the Professor's pen an elaborate argument, aiming to show that the successful teaching of Negroes "proves absolutely nothing,"—but a little further down his logical page he added, "it proves conclusively" that the superior genius of the white man enables him to teach an "inferior" anything that the white man knows. The article consisted almost entirely of such *conclusive* logic.

But now the Professor is hard to draw into these discussions, and is generally evasive in his answers and commonplace in his statements. He has been popular ever since he was elected to his professorship over a number of able competitors,—some of his beaten rivals being mean enough to assert that his first name (Jefferson Davis) recommended him to the trustees more than did his scholarship. Whether that be truth or slander, it is known that he almost always, and especially when appealing for support or favor, writes his full name,—*Jefferson Davis Jones.*

But to the cause of the Professor's lack of enthusiasm now when the Negro is being discussed— a dicussison so dear and interesting to a Southern gathering when the Negro is shut out. Last summer the Profesor by sheer accident ran head-on into a *fact*,—one of those hard rocks of experience against which the ships of theory have ever been and will ever be wrecked. This fact was a real Negro, a six-foot black man named Nathan Turner, employed at the wharf of the Munson Steamship Line. The eminent anthropologist and cognominal descendant of the President of the Confederacy had never seen or known so much of the Negro race in all the four decades of his life as he learned thru contact with "the Turner nigger" in less than four days.

Nathan Turner had been the talk of the "clubs" about six months before; at which time he had been given the remarkably light fine of twenty-five dollars in cash and thirty days on the chain gang for disarming and whipping a white man who had drawn a gun to shoot him, and the white man had been severely reprimanded by the court for allowing himseslf to be drawn into a fight with an "inferior and vicious character" instead of appealing to the officers of the law: for a policeman who was at the scene of trouble as an onlooker was not invited by the white man to take a hand in the affray until the "vicious character" had disarmed him and thrown him to the ground, when the vigilant officer at the call of the vanquished gentleman rushed in, used his mace bloodily on the Negro's head and hauled him off to the lock-up. This "vicious" defence made by the Negro together with the light sentence placed upon him and the severe reprimand imposed upon the white man, almost caused the black man to be lynched on the following night.— But a recorder's court in Mobile is no fool, and like many other courts in similar cases the recorder did not render judgment on the real issue, on the things that were seen and witnessed: for most of the eye-witnesses were on Nathan Turner's side, and one of them was his white employer, Captain Henry Sims. So the court admitted into evidence an obscure and crumpled piece of paper on which some "Nathan Turner" had written to some unknown person that there was a certain white man whom he meant to whip if he ever bothered him again. It was asserted by the lawyer of the white "complainant" (for the Negro is always the "defendant" in such a case) that the "said Nathan Turner" was the author and his client the victim of this threat. Finally Turner secured the privilege of writing his own name for the inspection of the court to show that he was not the author of the document in question. He signed habitually: "Nat. Turner." The court, who had been reared and schooled in a certain part of South Carolina where the famous insurrectionary slave is still execrated, was seen to frown like a storm, then redden like lightning and literally thunder out: "Nigger, is your name 'Nat Turner'?"—completely ignoring the period. The unsuspecting black man replied· "People sometimes call me that, and I sign it that way for short." "Well," thundered his honor again—and the lightning struck, "you're guilty—twenty-five dollars and thirty days!"

What is in a name? Is man fated from his birth and christening? Just as Prof. Jefferson Davis Jones's praenomina had been suspected to be among his assets in life, so now Nathan Turner's signature, tho absolutely different from the one that had been ascribed to him, proved to be among his liabilities. Captain Sims, who was also a native

Southerner but who had had much experience with actual instead of imaginary Negroes, was literally white with anger at this style of justice, but was impotent. He bestirred himselsf, however, to avert the lynching that the newspapers predicted for that night; and in the face of sharp criticism he re-employed Nathan Turner at the wharf as soon as his term was finished on the chain gang.

The anthropological Professor and this real Negro, two men of historic names, were destined to share together an intensely human experience,— where Nature herself becomes the judge, and in which names are really of no account and the fact of individual superiority or inferiority rises to such prominence as to entirely obscure all considerations of race or color.

Captain Sims, a fellow-clubman of the Professor, invited him to go on a few days outing,— camping, fishing and shooting near the end of Mobile Bay. The Captain owned some land on an island near Fort Gaines and had a gasoline launch which he often used on these excursions. On an outing of several days he always took his trusted employee, the black man whom he had befriended, Nathan Turner.

Turner was given a week's vacation and hired to accompany the two white men on a two or three days' excursion around outside the bay where the Captain had often found good sport. The usual equipment was taken, including several glass jugs of water and enough food for two or three days. The weather was beautiful and the waters smooth, and the Captain yielded to the temptation to bear rather far out and enjoy the open sea; and they got completely out of call and almost out of sight of land. Altho Turner was busily engaged in manipulating the boat, he could hear some of the conversation between the two white men. Their talk drifted thru various subjects into politics, and thence straight to the *inevitable*, the Race Question. As is the habit in the South they frankly expressed their opinions of the Negro race regardless of the ears of Turner (for he gave no attention whatever with his eyes), as if they did not consider him a part of the thing they were discussing.

To be sure the Captain disagreed politely with many of the opinions of the Professor, and stoutly asserted that, having known many Negroes personally, he believed that they did exactly what white people would do if on the same plane and in the same circumstances. And with the characteristic concessions and apologies of a white man in the Captain's position, he readily explained that he by no means thought the Negro to be the white man's equal and did not believe in "social equality," —but that he thought the Negro, even tho inferior, should be given justice, and that the very fact of his inferiority should make it easier to do him justice, inasmuch as he could not be feared as a rival. Then like a plain man of common sense, he tried to finish the argument by a direct parallel with the lower animals, and glancing at Turner, who was all ears but no eyes, he continued: "Now take the horse,—we are really not afraid of horses, therefore we do not make laws against them nor allow them to be lynched. Why, if the most vicious horse in this state should be brought out into the public square, chained to a post and burned alive, this whole damned country would go wild. Somebody would certainly get into jail and be ostracised from good society if not sent to the penitentiary,—and every preacher in Alabama would rant about it for months. But you put the best nigger in Mobile in the place of that horse and most people in this country will excuse it if they don't defend it."

For a plain mind like that of Sims this was an unanswerable argument, but not so for the anthropological mind. The Professor belonged to that class who may be convinced but cannot be converted. He was like the politician who remarked that he had heard many arguments that could convince his reason, but that he had never yet heard one that could influence his vote. And so he replied that he did not believe in "unnecessary" killing of Negroes, but that the white race's "instincts of self-preservation and sympathy of kind" would naturally lead it into excesses whenever it was threatened to be "overwhelmed and submerged by an inferior element." And without deigning to explain how a superior ten could ever be "over-

whelmed" by an inferior *one*, he went on to say
that the Negro is vicious and treacherous and is
always really waiting to get the advantage of the
white race.—All this was said right in the ears of
Turner, as if he were indeed a lower animal and
without capacity to perceive his own relation to the
discussion.

"Well," rejoined the Captain, "I don't know much
about theories but I know a few facts. Take the
case of Nathan Turner here. I have known him
nearly all his life, and he is one of the best work-
men in every sense of the word that we have ever
had; but a few months ago, you remember, all the
papers of Mobile called him a desperado and
threatened him with lynching. And he would have
been lynched if I had not persuaded the sheriff
to———"

He was interrupted by a popping followed by a
sharp explosion from the gasoline engine. In a
moment the Captain and Turner were searching
about the machine to see what had happened.
"This pipe is bu'sted and the plug blown out," said
Turner. As the Captain stooped to look he slipped
and caught on his hand. "What in the hell is that?"
he exclaimed, looking at his gashed and bleeding
hand, "has the dern thing broken all the water
jugs?"—For he had fallen on a fragment of glass.
—"No," answered Turner, "here is one jug not
broken."

After a brief examination of the damage to the

machine, it was seen to be absolutely beyond their means of repair.

"Nathan, how far out are we?" asked Captain Sims.

"About a half dozen miles, I think," replied Turner.

"Well," said Sims to the somewhat startled professor, "it is after four o'clock, so we are in for it."

With the characteristic confidence of the human mind they expressed the opinion that some vessel would pass in hailing distance before night and pick them up or tow them in.—The explosion evidently broke the Professor's chain of logic, for he was less talkative; or perhaps he was remembering the time when he had heard of this Turner Negro before and of his daring to whip a white man,— and how he himself at the University Club had been inspired by the incident to discourse anthropologically on the Negro race and to denounce Turner as "one of those vicious brutes who ought not to be at large." At any rate the suspicion arose in his mind that perhaps this Negro out of resentment to what he had overheard caused the machinery to break on purpose, and he hinted that suspicion to Sims. But the Captain who in his present predicament was not so patient with anthropology as he had been, gave him an emphatic "No" and added almost curtly that he would trust Nathan as far as he would any white man of his acquaintance.

At six in the evening they ate lunch and drank

water, still expecting succor. Consistent with the customs of their civilization the Negro was doled out a portion after the white men had entirely finished.

After lunch they all waited in silence, as if each hesitated to confess to the others his waning hope for being picked up that night. Turner broke the silence between seven and eight by calling attention to a rising cloud in the northwest and the stiffening breeze. He suggested that they unroll the tarpaulin and fasten it over the boat as a precaution against rain and perhaps spray. Hardly had they done this when half of the sky was covered with cloud and the wind was causing small whitecaps on the waves. It was evident that they were being blown further and further out to sea. The sky grew darker, the wind blew harder. They were, of course, helpless as to whither they were drifting, but Turner took the rudder and "trimmed" the boat as best he could to keep it from capsizing and to keep the water out, meanwhile issuing orders to his comrades in danger as if he had become their commander by appointment of Nature. These orders were implicitly obeyed and instructions even asked for by the other two men. Perhaps the Professor consoled himself with the useful logic that there is no use in standing upon technicalities since all men are the same color in the dark.

After being driven and beaten about all night in terror of their lives, soaked with sea water, they met in the morning a dead calm almost as suddenly as they had encountered the storm on the evening before. The Professor looked ten years older than yesterday, with his bedraggled longish hair and clean-shaven sallow face. "I wonder where in the world we are," he ejaculated.

"We must be somewhere in the middle of the Gulf, judging by the rate at which we were blown along," said Captain Sims, feigning courage by his exaggeration. "I suppose we need food after such a hard fight, but we must be careful with bread and water, for we may need what we have for several days yet." So saying he arranged three small lunches, and as if the wind had really blown them far enough from the center of their peculiar civilization to allow them immunity from its stern mandates and iron customs, he said: "Come on, Nathan, let's all eat.—I don't know what would have happened without Nathan; his head is as cool as the wind."

The dead calm continued; the sky became clear and the day warm. All day and all night and until the middle of the next day they waited, but nothing human was seen above their horizon outside the bounds of their little boat. The sea was almost like glass for smoothness and the sky was hot and hazy. There was not much food; some of it got wet and spoiled; and the water was getting low in the jug, tho they partook of it very sparingly. They had planned so that one of them was awake all the time on the lookout for succor, and Nathan Turner did most of the Captain's watching, for the latter was rather sick and suspected ptomaine poisoning.

On the afternoon of this second day following the storm the Negro several times noticed the two white men in secret and earnest conversation in which the Professor seemed to be the aggressor and the Captain the objector. The quick instinct of the Negro led him to suspect that this conversation in some way related to him,—for what other secret could interest two white men in the present situation? At one time when they had their heads together he noticed them direct their eyes and evidently their conversation to the small quantity of water in the jug. Later in the afternoon he saw the Captain frown and say to the importunate Professor something of which Turner could catch only the last words,—"saved us already and may be our dependence yet." Turner was not certain whether these words referred to him or to the water,—but in either case he concluded that the scarcity of food and water was the cause of the anxiety, and that inasmuch as the conversation was secreted from him it must be his share in these necessaries that was under debate. White people usually discuss the Negro's share with the Negro absent.

So far his reasoning was correct, but it might have alarmed him had he guessed what stern measure the Professor was urging the Captain to em-

ploy in order to secure the Negro's share of bread
and water for themselves, in the hope that even a
day or an hour more of life might cause the two
of them to be saved. He noticed, however, that
the guns and hunting knives were kept close under
the white men's eyes when not under their very
hands. Turner had always trusted the Captain,
but there gradually arose in his mind the suspicion,
which is pretty general among the members of his
race, that in a case like this the best white man
cannot be expected to do justice to a black man.
Besides, Sims was growing sicker and weaker until
by night he was quite helpless. Turner made him
a "pallet" by spreading a blanket in the rear of the
boat and folding the sick man's coat for a pillow.

Now for the night Turner and the Professor,
whom he thoroly distrusted by this time, must
take turns in the watching. What should he do
when his turn came to sleep?—He decided upon a
simple ruse: to feign sleep in his turn and watch
the Professor's movements. So, taking the first
watch and keeping it till nearly midnight he noticed
that the Professor did not sleep or slept very light-
ly, for he stirred whenever Turner made any unusual movement. As is the rule, this suspicion by
the white man made the Negro more suspicious of
the white man.

In these two human bosoms a desperation was
growing. .Tho their tongues were silent as the
tomb, their spirits communed together in bitter-

ness. Each suspected that the other understood him: and tho no threatening word had been uttered nor hostile hand raised they were already engaged in a spiritual death-struggle.

At last Turner said unconcernedly: "I'll rest now, if you'll watch."

"All right," said the anthropologist, with a sigh, as if he had been holding his breath.

Turner sat leaning back against the front of the boat and became quiet; his heart beat jerkily and his muscles tightened as he observed the other man move stealthily toward the rear where lay two dangerous incentives,—food and weapons. But feigning sleep brought no decisive result. Finally he became half unconscious with weariness and watching, when a slight tremor of the boat waked him. He threw up his hands and thrust something hard from before his face just as there was the "crack" of a 38-calibre rifle. He uttered an involuntary shriek of surprise, but only his left thumb which had caught the gun on the end, had been grazed and burnt by the discharge.

The sick man, startled into sudden strength by the report of the gun, shouted: "You damned fool! I told you not to kill him. The water would have lasted a day or two longer and he might have saved our lives."

But just then the sick man's eyes fell upon the most savage crisis in the animal world,—a hand-to-hand, man-to-man struggle. The two figures in the front of the boat with the weapon lifted high between them were writhing and twisting like silhouettes in a cinematograph. Foiled in his attempt, the Professor was now engaged in what he thought to be a death-struggle. No anthropological idea, if indeed one could have found lodgment in his tumultuous mind, could now bow his antagonist. Kipling has suggested that there is neither kith nor kin nor race nor breed nor birth, when two strong men stand face to face, "tho they come from the ends of the earth."—Finally one of the strugglers gave way with a despairing groan and the other tumbled forward upon him. The sick man was so exhausted with excitement that he could not even speak. "You sly coward!" shouted the voice of Nathan Turner. "If I were low-down like you now I'd throw you into the Gulf."

By right of conquest the Negro was now the master. "Don't be worried, Cap'n Sims," said he coldly. "I'll look after the Pr'fess'r." He then ordered the Professor to remain where he was, while he proceeded to throw overboard all the weapons except a sheathed hunting knife which he put on his own person. Then saying, "I'm sorry, Mister, but I want to keep you out of trouble and I want to stay out of trouble myself," he securely tied the Professor's hands behind his back and left him on watch while he himself went to rest.

The Negro secretly admired what he called in his mind the "gameness" of the white man in that he did not waste words in protest or make futile resistance after he found himself completely worsted.

As day broke the Captain said that he was feeling better and asked for a little water. Turner gave him a drink and then asked the silent Professor in a searching, conciliatory voice if he did not want a drink also. He replied coldly that he would like to have a drink, "if you are willing to give me any." Paying no attention to the conditional clause, Turner poured out some water, and as he was about to raise the cup to the other man's mouth, he stopped and said: "Now, there ain't a bit of use in this sort of foolishness. We are all in the same boat. We may go to the bottom and we may be saved, but we can all be fair to one another. I can forget all about our little difference last night if you can."

The white man hesitated for a minute as if searching for an expedient in an embarrassing situation, and then said: "I will be willing to do whatever you and Captain Sims think best."

"All right," said Turner, ignoring the irrelevant part of the reply, and untying the prisoner, "I think it best for us all to go along together, and I think we are going to be picked up before to-morrow night."

Captain Sims, who had tactfully taken no notice of these proceedings, remarked that he believed he discerned smoke to the southward. The others strained their eyes but were not certain of any smoke. But an hour later they saw a small steamer to the southwest of them, evidently headed northwest. Immediately Turner sprang on the bow of the launch and waved his hat and shouted with all his might. They all shouted and waved frantically, but seemingly in vain, for no heed was taken of them. Finally Turner literally tore off his shirt which he tied to a fishing rod; this he handed to the Professor, and lifting him into the air told him to wave it. A few minutes of this strenuous exercise caused a puff of steam to fly up from the ship, and a moment later the hoarse whistling reached them. She changed her course, a boat and crew were lowered and the rescued men were taken aboard with their launch.—It was a Cuban crew, and Captain Sims knew enough Spanish to learn that they were going from Havana to New Orleans.

Four days later there appeared in the Mobile Evening News an account of the harrowing experience of two prominent white citizens and a Negro wharf employee named Nathan Turner. The Negro was the only one mentioned by name, and great stress was laid on his "exceptional" courage and his commendable "faithfulness" to the two white men.

Captain Sims chuckled as he showed this "peace offering" to Nathan Turner, who laughed and opened his white eyes, making his inky-black face look even blacker, when he saw himself described as a "dark mulatto,"—for they both knew that **the** contributing editor of the News was Professor Jefferson Davis Jones.

"PASSING THE BUCK"

The North and the South met together at the great Methodist Centenary Exposition in Columbus Ohio. An unusual practice of democracy was prevalent there, when we consider that fact. All the races of mankind mingled freely in the various privileges of the exposition. The reactionaries were there, however, and they only tolerated this democracy; they did not indorse it.

Among these was a group of four persons from a moderate-sized North Carolina town, who had been "suckled on a creed outworn,"—the creed of inherent racial superiority. One was the mother, proud in her graying light hair, consistent daughter of a former slave-holding aristocracy. There was the daughter of this matron, a real Southern belle, with light hair slightly fluffy rather than curly, twenty years old, aquiline, lithe, well-shaped, with small feet and lean ankles. There was the son and brother, twenty-six years old, smelling of cigarettes, brusque in manner, drawling in speech, and swearing easily. The fourth was a nephew and cousin, who was born and reared in Ohio, from Abolitionist stock on his father's side, but who had now been living in the South with his cousins just long enough to become "converted" and subverted on the race question. He had learned to "hate niggers" as only a Southernized Northerner can. It had taken him just thirteen months to learn that the North was "all wrong" on the Negro and the South. Thirteen months of contact in the South had undone thirty-odd years of training in Christian democracy in his father's house and at Oberlin College.

This "converted" Northerner was becoming very popular in that North Carolina community. His street-corner confessions of a change of heart, and his ready ridicule of the sentimentality of his Northern home folk had advertised him as a "sensible Yankee." If he would make his home in North Carolina, local people told him, he could get to Congress on the Democratic ticket and "help to open the eyes of the North."

It was especially urged by the leaders of the Southern church that this converted man should go to the Centenary Celebration in Columbus, where they would arrange for him to appear among the speakers and begin at once his mission of enlightening those benighted people still left in isolated places of the North who believe that "niggers" are human beings.

At the exposition grounds this party of four had got acquainted with another man from Ohio, who was much attracted by the physical beauty and vivacity of the Southern belle. This Ohioan was a faithful churchman, with his business in Cincinnati and his home in one of the smaller towns between that city and Columbus. He enjoyed the company of the Southern party, dined with them, and together they visited the various exhibits during the last two weeks of the exposition. After they had passed through the exhibit section called "THE AMERICAN NEGRO," he was amused at their views concerning the colored race, which they continued to force into the conversations, in spite of his efforts to change the subject. Many Southern white people feel it like a patriotic duty to make converts on this subject.

Finally one day as they sat by "the lake" under the trees at the exposition grounds the discussion was waxing hot on the topic as to whether any Negro, however intelligent and seemingly refined, should ever be regarded and treated as a gentleman by white people. The simple-minded and unsophisticated Northerner ventured to offer evidence of this kind: "Why, I know one, have known him for ten years. He is an assistant clerk in our Cincinnati office. He was a southern boy, who graduated with honors at Yale and has made good. He is a real gentleman. I saw him today, I will introduce him to you just to let you see for yourselves."

The way in which the quartet greeted this last suggestion of his made this well-meaning

man feel silly and sick. The belle laughed at
him openly as if he were a fool. Her brother
swore mutteringly. The "converted" cousin
hissed and sneered. And the mother, with all
the conscious pride of three hundred years of
active "race superiority," threw back her head
and said: " Why we have in our own state
hundreds of niggers who are just as intelligent
as the one you speak of, but they are *niggers* just
the same,—and nobody ever presumed to 'introduce' them to us !"

The simple-hearted offender somewhat confused,
said hurriedly: "I do not mean to encroach upon
your private rights,—but he is a friend of mine."
At this the women smiled, the brother guffawed,
and the "converted" one remarked: "You need to
come South,—that's what you need."

"One nigger had the nerve," said the brother,
"to sit right down at our table when we were eating in the cafeteria."--"And then," said the mother,
"he also had the nerve to come over to the Colis-
eum and take a seat right in front of *me!*"

"That's not all," remarked the "converted"
cousin, "but I remembered that darkey's face,
and he is the same fellow that heckled me when
I spoke at the Big Tent this afternoon."

What really happened in the Big Tent was this:
About three thousand Celebration visitors had gath-
ered there to hear a speech announced as: "The
Confessions of an Ohioan from North Carolina."

Black and white, North and South, gathered to hear these "confessions." In justice to the majority of those in charge of the Celebration, it should be said that this speech would never have been allowed, had its real nature been anticipated. The "converted" Northerner made the worst anti-Negro speech that had been uttered since Wilson muzzled Vardaman and the Lord muzzled Tillman. He said that Negroes should not vote, that "blood would run" (especially in North Carolina) before they would submit to the official rule of any Negro, that the Negro was only after "'social equality,'" etc. To prove the last statement he instanced that a few Negro babies had been left in France by colored American soldiers! At this point the colored man's voice called out from the rear of the tent: "And how do you explain the millions of mulattoes in the South?" The blow temporarily stunned the speaker, and as he recovered he replied: "Er—ah—er I'm coming to that later." He never came to it.

The speaker did not seem to realize that in France there was no social barrier,—and that there *is* a barrier in the South, set by white men themselves; and that therefore the association of black men with white women in France, where there is no barrier, was *virtue*, as compared with the *viciousness* of the American white man who breaks through the very barrier which he has hypocritically set up to preserve his own "racial integrity." There

are many people who have not considered that difference.

At the close of the Celebration this party of four
decided to visit Cincinnati on their way back to the
South. The Northern acquaintance had seen them
to the station and into the Cincinnati sleeper, and
as the train did not leave till after midnight, he
had promised, if possible, to get a ticket for that
same train, or else to come next day and show
them about Cincinnati. He had some business en-
gagement in Columbus which he could not be sure
of getting rid of that evening.

As he was leaving the gate at the Union Station, he met his colored friend going in to take
the train for Cincinnati. "If you had got here a
little earlier I could have introduced you to those
Southern friends of mine, who, I told you, are so
anxious to meet you." Both laughed.

"Let me see your ticket," continued the white
friend. "By the way, you are in their car. Too
bad you have not had an introduction. I must
hurry now and try to take that car myself."

Meanwhile the Southern party had found its
berths. The mother had lower seven, the daughter
lower eight opposite, and the men had nine and
ten. When the colored man entered the car, the
daughter had put her coat and bag on the seat at
section eight, but was herself sitting in nine talking to the two men.

There is humor in fate. This colored man walk-

ed straight to number eight and deposited his belongings and took his seat. He had the upper.
When the two men saw him, they were like bulls
when they see a red rag. There was brief con-
sternation and then some half audible "damns"
only indirectly aimed at the colored passenger, and
to which he paid no seeming attention whatever.
He continued to read a newspaper. He rather felt
than saw them as they ostentatiously came over and
removed the girl's belongings to one of the men's
berths and brought a man's coat and bag and flung
them defiantly into number eight. In order to
strengthen his wilful indifference by action, the
colored man got up and moved off unconcernedly
to the smoking room. As he went he overheard
one say: "that same old nigger ——." He began
to recollect, and the cafeteria and the Big Tent
came up in his mind.

When he returned from the smoking room later,
he found the girl's belongings back in number
eight, and she and the two men were chatting
merrily and normally in a nearby seat, as if
nothing had ever happened. This made him suspicious. It is strange that normal conduct, coming
as a quick successor to abnormal conduct, will invariably make us suspect. He began to think, and
later he moved off again to the smoking room and
thought and thought some more.

After a while the porter came into the smoking

room and said: "All berths have been made down, sir, when you are ready to retire."

"Wait here a minute, porter," said the colored man, "I have something to say to you." He first stepped out and peeped in at the berths. What he saw confirmed his suspicions. The cousin and brother were in earnest conversation with the Southern girl. She appeared to be objecting instinctively, but they seemed to be urging it, almost compelling her. An agreement seemed to be reached, the girl yielding very reluctantly, and each turned to his own berth, she going to number eight.

The colored passenger went back to the smoking room: "Porter, here's a dollar. I want you to do something for me,—very little trouble to you. And I will explain before we reach Cincinnati. Tell the conductor that I am an old friend of yours; that I want to sit up here with you and talk over old times; and that he need not refund my money for upper eight unless some other passenger takes it. But listen, porter, don't you let any colored person get into it. I'll claim it myself first. Put some white man into it, especially if a tall young fellow in a Palm Beach suit asks for accommodations to Cincinnati."

The porter stared a bit, seemingly mystified, but finally shrugged his shoulders and said: "I'll fix that all right."

Later the porter was heard to say to some one on the platform: "No, sir, all space is taken. You might try the St. Louis car." Later, still, to some other applicant: "Yessir, yessirree, jes' one upper left, sir. You goin' to Cincinnati?" The porter's voice seemed to be intentionally loud. The colored passenger slipped into the toilet room. He heard the new arrival come into the smoking room, wash his hands and go off with the porter to climb into his berth. The porter returned.

"Was it he, porter?"

"Yes, it's him. Gone to upper eight."

"Anybody see him?"

"No. The lights are out and all seem sleep."

Soon the Pullman conductor came in, looked at his watch, yawned and remarked to the colored passenger: "Porter seems glad to see one of his old friends; it's been a long *dry* spell in Ohio,"— and then he chuckled at his own wit.

After he and the colored passenger and the porter had talked about a number of things and the train was on its way, a slight commotion was heard in the berth sections, with confused voices. The colored passenger covertly touched the porter's arm and kept him back while the Pullman conductor went to investigate. When the conductor went in, the excited voices became louder: "If you don't have him arrested, conductor, and put off this train, we'll fix him. He ought to be in North Carolina—that's what I say about lettin' niggers into Pullman cars—we know 'em in

the south all right——," the two men seemed to
be awfully wrought up.

Meanwhile the colored passenger, in the smoking room, had given the porter some hurried ex-
planations. The porter turned on the lights and
they two went and peeped in. Three persons were
in the aisle remonstrating with the conductor, two
men and a woman, they in their trousers, and she
in her kimono, looking really and truly excited.

"Come here, porter,". shouted the conductor.
Then to the two men: "Well, we won't have any
personal violence done in this car. So you just
put up that gun and we'll get the train conductor
and investigate."

"Investigate hell! you'll put that nigger out o'
here or we will!"

Meanwhile the porter had gone for the train
conductor. The colored passenger was peeping in,
still unobserved. When the train conductor came,
the Pullman conductor hastily explained, conclud-
ing: "—— and they charge that the passenger in
the upper annoyed her."

"He started into her berth," said the brother.

"Wait!" said the conductor, and he shook the
mattress of upper eight.

"He's not asleep," sneered one of the Southern-
ers.

The conductor shook again, and a truly sleepy
voice said: "Is it time to get up?"

"The hell it is!" snarled the brother.

"Wake up," said the conductor, "you are charged with trying to enter the berth of the lady in lower eight."

"Well," said the voice now fully awake, "I'm a church member, but whoever made that charge is a damned liar!" And with that a tousled red head shot out from between the green curtains.

The girl fainted.

The brother said: "There must be some mistake."

The red head rubbed its eyes and said: "What in God's name?"

"Where's the nigger?" asked the cousin. "It was a nigger, she meant."

Heads were sticking out from several berths by this time and at this juncture our colored passenger walked in from the smoking room.

"There he is," said the brother.

"He?" said the Pullman conductor, "I left him in the smoking room with the porter when I heard the racket and came in here, and he had been there talking to me and the porter ever since the train started."

The colored passenger looked on scornfully, with his lips tight.

"Well!" shouted the disgusted train conductor, "this passenger in upper eight—has *he* done anything?"

"No!" yelled the "converted" one, in great humiliation and anger.

The conductor wheeled and left. The mother accompanied her reviving daughter to the women's room.

"She'll explain," said the profane brother in an embarrassed voice to the head in upper eight.

By this time, however, the man in the upper and the colored passenger had caught each other's eye, and the latter was remarking: "*I* will explain to *you* tomorrow at the office."

The next afternoon at the office in Cincinnati, after they had expressed their mutual disgust at the experiences of the night before, the colored assistant clerk remarked to his friend: "I saw that a rather intimate relationship was going to develop, and knowing that you were an acquaintance of theirs, and not having yet had the honor of an introduction myself, I decided to *pass the buck to you!*"

TIT FOR TAT

How Colored Soldiers Defeated the Real Enemy at Grand Villars

This is one of the true stories of the war. And true stories are really the more fascinating.

The colored soldiers in this case were the 370th regiment, largely from Chicago and the South, and the "real enemy" was a white American regiment that was full of Negro-haters.

The people of the little French town of Grand Villars are of the simple-living, noble-minded peasant class, with high ideals of human life and free from many of the petty motives that spoil much of the rest of the world. They had never seen Americans, and it happened that the first American soldiers stationed among them were colored, the 370th. This regiment was such a good sample of its own colored people in America, running thru all the possible colors from white Negroes to black. And yet they were of one heart and soul and mind, and when they marched down the streets of Grand Villars, clothed in khaki, they looked like one solid block of animated invincible bronze.

It was perfectly natural that these French people should take this first sample as a type of all Americans. That first impression of the "Americain" became fixed. They thought, and not altogether incorrectly, that the American people were of many varying human hues, and they thought that COLOR predominated.

They also thought, perhaps less correctly, that all Americans had the spirit of these boys: polite, gentle to women, and hearty to all men. The most ordinary peasant woman was treated by these colored soldiers with the same civility which they accorded to the fashionable French women of the town. A colored captain says that he would see several French girls with water buckets on their arms and pushing baby carriages as they descended the hill to the spring; but that when these girls returned from the spring, each bucket would be carried and each baby carriage pushed by some big stalwart soldier of the 370th.

The people of Grand Villars thought that America must be a place of wonderful democracy! Curiously enough the colored soldier was the best ally of Woodrow Wilson, and caused the French people to believe the words that emanated from the White House.

Naturally the whole town, men, women and children, took this regiment right into its heart; no door was closed to them; nothing was for them too good or quite good enough. As they anchored the hopes of the French by their soldierly bearing, so also did they gladden the hearthsides with their tales and songs. The girls were charmed when the colored boys exhibited the photographs and extolled the fine points of "the browns" they had left behind.—Well, as long as man is man, there will always arise out of such agreeable society what arose here—genuine love. The people loved these boys, and these boys loved the people.

And then it happened. A white American regiment came and encamped five miles from Grand Villars. These soldiers of one monotonous hue, were less attractive to strangers than the varicolored men of the 370th. Then, too, they were not so polite; they were colder to the men, and more assuming and direct among the women and girls. They did not say so evenly to rich and poor alike the euphonious French "good morning" and "good evening,"—*bonjour* and *bonsoir!* And when these white Americans went into the homes of the people, after chatting awhile with the young ladies, they might notice on the table the photograph of a brown or black soldier: "What is this?"

A girl would reply: "O, Monsieur, that is my John or (Sam, or Jake, or whatever happened to be the name of that particular member of the 370th), *mon bon ami!*" (my beau).

Then hostilities began.

"Your *what?* Why, don't you know that no white person ever associates with them in America? They

are not allowed to enter our homes or to speak to
any white woman. When a white woman in the
United States just speaks to one of those fellows,
all other white people shut her out of their homes
and never speak to her again!"

The white fellows very naturally laid it on a
little thick, in their efforts to cause the puzzled
French listeners to grasp the significance of this
peculiar thing.

"They are not Americans; they are just *niggers*.
We only allow them to live in our country because
their people were once slaves there. But they are
not American citizens and are not even allowed
to talk back to white people. And they are very
criminal and dishonest; they will steal. They are
especially dangerous to women: in our country no
white woman dares to go near them unless a white
man is with her."

And just like most falsehoods, right there is
where it over-shot the mark and laid the foundation
for its own undoing; for the girls of the house might
be seen to look at each other, indicating that they
themselves knew this last to be false. But in spite
of their own experiences with these brown boys,
they were somewhat disturbed by this brazen attack. Human nature can hardly trust itself. We
are all more or less at the mercy of what we hear,
—until we begin to *confer*. So, when the girls of
the town would gather in little groups, one would
break the ice with a whisper: "Those new Ameri-

cans tell me that my John is bad." Then other girls would pipe in:

"And they told mama that my Sam is bad."—"And they tell father that my Bill is bad."—"And they say that mine is bad."—"And mine."

And strange to say, the very unanimity of the report raised the first confident doubt of it; and more than one would remark: "Well, it must be a falsehood, *for it is impossible that they all should be bad!*" Such is the training of the French mind that it could only think of goodness or badness as belonging to individuals, and could not attach a moral idea to race or color. They could not grasp the idea of a bad race, and they thought of worth or unworth as an individual characteristic.

After getting this encourgement from each other, the girls began to confide the matter to their colored friends.

The colored boys then got their heads together, and in strict compliance with the laws of human nature, they began to plan for defense and counter-attack. A strategem was conceived by one of their lieutenants and he proposed to call all the girls and women of Grand Villars to assemble in convention and hear a speech from him. When the summons went forth, the whole town came out. For because of the good behavior of their men, the officers of the 370th regiment literally "owned the town."

The lieutenant took the platform. He had grown

up in New Orleans and could speak excellent French. And this is the barage which he laid down against the attacking enemy:

"Women and girls of Grand Villars: We regret to find it necessary to give you fair warning. You have seen for yourselves that the soldiers who are encamped near this village are not *real* Americans, altho they are enlisted in the American Army. Americans are polite: they are not. Americans are cordial: they are cold. Americans are gentle: they are rough. Americans are democratic: these men are snobbish. Americans respect alike the honorable rich and the honest poor: these men worship money but respect nobody. Americans do not like to disparage their fellow countrymen or their comrades-in-arms: these men have tried without cause to slander us. Americans are brave: these men are not brave, for they do not face us, but they attack us in secret to you.

"Now it is my painful duty to tell you who these men are. Without protest we allow them to live in our country, but they hate us. We are just to them and treat them as men,—as equals before the law; but they are unjust to us and assume an attitude of natural superiority. Many of them are descendants of the German and the Austrian, and have much of the old arrogance of their forefathers. Because of their conduct we do not associate with them in our country, and we do not

call them Americans: we call them—er— 'crackers'
and 'pecks'!"

That was a finisher. The soldiers of the five-
mile camp were chagrined and "stung" to find the
private doors of Grand Villars tightly closed to
them, while the 370th enjoyed greater hospitality
than ever before. It was a pitiable sight,—this
complete and sincere ostricism of the haughty and
the proud. It was a heavy dose of their own medicine,—the most terrible thing that could be offered
them. If any treatment could cure a man, it
should be that. True to their sympathetic nature,
the colored boys became really sorry for the white
boys, when they saw them in groups on the street
corners, looking in vain for society and sympathy,
—and sometimes tarrying so late that the military
guard would have to order them out at the gate.
To be sure they could visit the public restaurants
and hotels; and the French waitress, when she
would pass a table where a colored soldier was
seated, would stoop low and whisper (not being
able to remember the longer epithet): "There are
a lot of those Pecks here tonight."

* * * * * *

The proof that our race prejudice is artificial,
abnormal and rather contrary to nature, is the fact
that an uninitiated mind like that of the French
simply cannot "understand" it. It was comical to
see them trying to "get it," when the white American was trying to explain. Some colored soldiers

were eating in the main dining room of an hotel
White American officers entered, and seeing a
smaller, less elegant dining room adjoining, they
called the proprietor and asked him to put the
colored soldiers in the smaller room, explaining
that they were "not fit" to eat with white men,
etc. You should have seen the face of this bewildered Frenchman, as he endeavored to be polite
and tried at the same time to square his common-
sense with this American puzzle: "Zhentlemen, I
do not understand. These other zhentlemen have
paid their bills and they are polite, and you say
they are not good enough to eat where you eat,—
I *do* not understand. These men are American
soldiers like you and have uniforms like you,—
I *do* not understand,—how can they be good enough
to be in the same uniform and not good enough to
eat in the same room? I *do* not understand. And,
my good zhentlemen, I will not compel you to eat
with the other zhentlemen,—the little dining room
is open, there is no one in it. why don't you go
into it? I cannot ask the others to move, for they
are satisfied. You are dissatisfied,—why should I
disturb the *satisfied one?* I *do* not understand!"

And on and on the bewildered Frenchman plead
before this inexorable American god. Small wonder it is that the average white American soldier
should lose some of his ardor for France after such
experiences. He was a puzzle to France, and
France must have been an enigma to him.—Per-

haps the only way in the world for the white American ever to appreciate this demon which he worships, is to have a chance to feel the full weight of his rod, as did the white soldiers at Grand Villars.

FINIS.